Operation Titan

'Far out beyond the orbit of the planet Saturn, space stretched endlessly, cold, dark and silent. Into the emptiness the mighty flagship *Conqueror* emerged, its wedge-shaped bulk slicing into the space-time continuum.

'Other craft appeared until finally a total of twelve warships powered in towards the speck that was Titan.'

The Empire rules by fear. It destroys all who oppose it. For the rebels on Titan escape seems impossible. In a desperate race against time, Paul Trentam sets out from Earth on a perilous rescue mission . . .

Dedicated with thanks to
Jonathan, Carol, Lance, George and Elizabeth

DILWYN HORVAT

OPERATION TITAN

A LION PAPERBACK

Oxford · Batavia · Sydney

Copyright © 1983 Dilwyn Edwin Horvat

Published by
Lion Publishing Corporation
1705 Hubbard Avenue, Batavia, Illinois 60510, USA
ISBN 0 7459 1731 3

First US edition 1989

Cover illustration: Peter Chiang

Library of Congress Cataloging-in-Publication Data

Horvat, Dilwyn.
    Operation Titan / Dilwyn Horvat. — 1st US ed.
       p.   cm. — (Lion paperback)
    Summary: The forces of the Empire plot to annihilate the
Christians living on Saturn's moon.
    ISBN 0–7459–1731–3
    [1. Science fiction.   2. Christian life—Fiction.]   I. Title.
PZ7.H792170p   1989
[Fic]—dc19   89–30303
                                                    CIP
                                                    AC

Printed and bound in Great Britain by
Cox & Wyman Ltd, Reading

Prologue

Space: silent and cold – the many moons of the Earth hung, glittering and bright, in their man-made orbits. Communications satellite SP Delta 5 clicked quietly to itself in anticipation of one of the only two events in its unremarkable day. Just over the horizon the sun was climbing inevitably towards the dawn. At precisely the expected moment an arc of white appeared at the rim of the globe and SP Delta 5 hummed in satisfaction. The twin solar panels tilted slightly to bask in the new-found light and, this done, all returned to the state of quiet watchfulness in which it had spent the night. No more was required of it for the next twelve hours when, its power cells fully recharged, the orbiter would sail on into the night, never pausing in the faithful service of its makers on the planet below.

Thousands of kilometers distant from the Earth, the fabric of space-time shifted momentarily to accommodate the bulk of a decelerating spacecraft, emerging from the timeless domain of hyperspace. In its cockpit, the pilot fought to keep control; fought against a slowly spreading paralysis of his left arm and the drowsy numbness of fatigue. A steady trickle of blood oozed from a wound high up in the left shoulder. As his eyes studied the instrument panel before him, he fought to keep back a creeping mist into which he was sinking and where he would find relief from the pain. For this reason the red light winking persistently at the periphery of his vision went unnoticed, and in its headlong plunge earthwards the craft encountered satellite SP Delta 5 sailing innocently through the same flight path.

The impact lasted less than a thousandth of a second. The two craft approached, met and separated in less time than that required to form an image in the pilot's mind. Behind, amidst a glittering halo of flying glass shards tumbling and flashing in the sunlight, hung the shattered remains of the satellite. Jolted from its orbit by the impact, it began a long, slow spiral earthwards.

At the controls of his craft, the pilot read the confusing array of alarms with a dim awareness. Behind and below him, the port directional stabilizer hung twisted and torn beneath the fuselage. The spaceship planed down through the upper atmosphere streaming a flare of molten metal from the gash in its belly. On board, the combined skills of human and computer pilots struggled to keep control and restrict the pitching spaceship to the narrow angle of approach that would guide it to the surface below. As the west coast of America passed beneath the speeding form, the pilot locked-in computer control and engaged the auto-eject system before finally yielding and sinking into the depths of unconsciousness.

Seconds later the bulk of the craft, mortally wounded by the rupture blazing white-hot beneath it, fragmented and plummeted earthwards. At the same instant, the cockpit section disengaged and blasted clear. Triple parachutes opened, checked the cabin in its descent before tearing free, reserve chutes replaced them, held, and slowed their charge in its flight. Minutes later, all that remained of the craft swung down into a small wooded area amidst splintering boughs and thudded to the ground, its precarious fall to earth completed.

As light began to fail before the approaching night, the cockpit canopy swung open. A hand appeared at the rim of the fuselage and the pilot hauled himself up from his seat to gaze dazedly around him. Taking over an hour to complete the task, and grunting with pain at each exertion, he dragged both himself and his companion clear

6

of the cabin. Then, exhausted, he lay back on the moss-covered earth and slept.

The moon rose high in the night sky, and its pale light filtered down through the trees to where the two lay. As the pilot slept on, his passenger stirred, mumbled incoherently in his drugged sleep, and then fell silent again. The boy was barely five years old.

1

The corridor curved away gently to the left. There were no windows. The lighting was pleasantly diffuse. His footsteps on the carpeting were almost silent. His pace was calmly measured; his gaze travelled freely over his surroundings, coolly observant. He passed several doorways. Each was marked by a red entry disc set into the adjacent panelling of the wall. He came to an intersection; immediately beyond it were two more doors, the second of which was his target. He crossed the open area, glancing neither to right nor left. There was no challenge. His pace slowed and he drew from his pocket a violet, gold-rimmed medallion. This he held against the disc by the doorway which slid open silently to admit him. He passed into the dark interior of the room and the entrance resealed behind him. He had not been seen.

He stood for a long moment in the darkness. The computer console stood invisible before him. His fingers felt for the touch panel and the room was filled with a comfortable light. He wheeled the chair away from the terminal and crouched beside the unit, withdrew a slim wallet from his breastpocket and selected the appropriate instrument. Under his expert attention the front panel came away to reveal the complexities of the circuitry within. He studied the stacks of electronic modules and after some time selected and withdrew one of the wafer-thin boards. This he replaced with a similar unit which he produced from his right-hand jacket pocket. He straightened and addressed the keyboard. The substitution he had just performed should now enable him to bypass its protected access system and gain entry to the computer core memory.

He paused as the filename request appeared on the screen. The next sequence he entered would, he knew, take him beyond the limits of general access and into the restricted files. If the unit he had manufactured and inserted into the machine failed to function, the security trip-system would operate, the whole computer complex would be sealed off and he would be helplessly trapped. He keyed-in the filename. The computer responded with a pause, the screen cleared and then filled with a page of information which he rapidly scanned. It worked.

He withdrew a mini disk from its cassette and inserted it into the drive on the console. He entered the copy sequence and watched as the text scrolled up the screen. Less than a minute later the disk was full and thirty-two pages copied. He began the reverse sequence to exit the memory, once again without alerting the security trip-system. The duplicate circuit board was replaced by the original and the front panel put back into position. He gathered the several items together and returned them to their original hiding-places within his clothing. A glance around the room confirmed that all was exactly as it had been when he entered. He turned out the light and waited. He could detect no sound other than the faint whisper of the air conditioning. The violet disc lay in the palm of his hand. He raised it to the level of the glowing red light in the wall. If anyone was within sight when he emerged from the room, he would be discovered. With a small click the enamelled surfaces met and the contact was made, the door slid open and he stepped out into the passage: empty. He retraced his steps. The elevator was still at his level. He entered and the door closed behind him. He pressed a button and began to slip down through the levels. He leaned against the wall, closed his eyes and breathed out deeply. Only now, as he relaxed, did a trace of perspiration appear on his brow. It had taken almost a year of preparation but now at last he knew his time had not been wasted.

He had beaten the security systems guarding the computer. The knowledge it contained was his for the taking. The disk in his jacket pocket was just the first of many. Soon they would know all they needed to know about the Knights and the filthy organization they protected. Using the information he would provide, the Empire would be able to deliver a decisive blow from which the Church would never recover. Overnight it would cease to exist. A smile broadened across his features and he fingered the purple medallion in his pocket. He would be richly rewarded.

In the control room, all eyes were fixed on the image on the wall. The silhouette of the approaching ship slipped and slid away from the center of the screen. The flight controller leaned forwards and spoke into his headset microphone.

'This is Ekklesia control. We have you on visual. Please steady your descent.'

'He's not going to make it.'

'Ground crew in position. We're ready for him.'

'Repeat, Orange 24; bring her in slowly.'

The old man's eyes narrowed as he traced the shadowy wisp trailing behind the incoming spacecraft.

'He's losing fuel . . .'

'If that ignites . . .'

'Launch area clear and sealed.'

The contrast of the picture changed. Along the undersurface of the craft details began to emerge from the greyness. He could make out what seemed to be a scorchmark running the whole length of its hull.

'Will you take a look at that?'

'Fire crew; are you getting this?'

'We see it.'

'Altitude 5.7 kilometers, approach vector 105 meters per second. He's coming in too fast.'

'Orange 24 to Ekklesia control. Making final approach. Instruments register fuel loss, do you copy?'

'We see it, 24. You are trailing vapor astern.' He covered the microphone with his hand and spoke to one side. 'Give me higher magnification; let's see where it's coming from.' The image changed and jerked giddily on the screen.

'Looks like the rear starboard thruster.'

'Hey, where is that thing?'

'You're right; it's gone, the whole engine's gone.'

'Can't they go into parking orbit till we can get someone up there and take a look at that?'

'No, cabin temperature's down, we've got to bring them in now. He probably couldn't stop anyway.' He spoke once more into the microphone. 'Source of fuel is rear starboard thruster; do not attempt to fire; do you copy?'

'Loud and clear, Ekklesia: rear starboard. You see anything else I should know about?'

They were still scanning the underneath of the plane, whose detail was now revealed in high relief. Damage was widespread but appeared to be superficial. The other three vertical thrusters that would be fired in the last stage of the descent appeared to have been spared.

'Other systems seem OK; you can make it. Still coming in a little fast; please correct.'

'Sealing off operations room.'

A faint tremor ran through the building. Heavy heat shields rose on every side until they met with the similarly-protected roof. The whole complex was enclosed. Even to those who had been through this drill many times before, it still felt uncomfortably like a tomb.

On board the incoming spacecraft, the pilot stared fixedly out of the flight-deck windows. The cabin was bathed in a dim red light. The bank of instruments to his right was a mass of tangled cables and splintered circuit boards; from somewhere inside came the sputter of short-circuiting electronics.

His copilot's voice came over the intercom. 'Cabin temperature still dropping; we're getting condensation.'

He fought to keep his grip on the control column steady; he was shivering violently inside his pressure suit. Crystalline patterns chased across the windscreen, forming, vanishing, reforming. At any instant, his line of sight was almost totally obscured.

'She's frosting over. I can't see a thing.'

A mist hung in the cabin. He wiped the visor of his helmet. For an instant he caught sight of the clustered minarets of Ekklesia; they were closing rapidly.

'See if you can do something about that ice.'

Several bulkheads further back down the ship, the human cargo lay in jumbled heaps. Individual forms were lost in the thick fog that filled the bay. A thin layer of frost crept inwards toward the stilled bodies and spread up and over the inner surface of the craft's metallic skin. The temperature was already well below zero; hands, faces were ashen grey, lips blue-tinged. The thinning air was leaking steadily through the micropunctures burned in the spaceship's hull. As the oxygen pressure continued to drop, each of the survivors sank deeper into unconsciousness. They were drawing close to death.

'OK; that's enough.' He was peering through a window where the copilot had scraped away the crust of frost. The temperature outside the cockpit was beginning to rise

13

as they approached the planet's surface. The patch remained clear. The spaceport beacon was clearly visible.

'Firing one, two and four.' He made to reach for the controls to his left and felt a tug at his wrist. His grip remained closed around the control column to which the glove of his suit had frozen. He became aware that there was no feeling in either hand.

'Carl, fire the thrusters; I can't move my hands.'

An arm reached across in front of him and he was thrown forwards against the seatbelt as the extra brake-power cut in. He felt the craft shudder around him. He eased the control column towards his body and the nose lifted in response. The vibration increased. The column kicked against his pull. They were now at low altitude, the spaceship responding ever more as a plane as they continued their descent. The air thickening around them was beginning to provide an appreciable drag. The pilot held the angle of attack steady just below stall despite the strain this was placing on his vessel.

The landscape rose to meet them, and as it did so the speed of their approach became more apparent. Familiar landmarks slipped by. Ahead, the glittering towers of Ekklesia shone in the daylight. The crystal city called to him across the void.

'Beginning landing sequence.' His gaze fixed on the beacon guiding him in.

'Ekklesia standing by.'

The spaceport complex lay ahead, a halo of lights ringing the launch area. He felt his hand come free of the control column and flexed his fingers. Tiny rivulets of melted ice ran down the windscreen.

'We're still coming in too fast. I'm increasing power.' He pushed forward the levers controlling the thruster engines past the red arrow marked overload and into the region beyond. They were now operating outside their design specifications with no safety margin; for how long, there was no way of knowing.

Their target was now seen to be the vast amphitheater it really was – a smooth, featureless granite-clad arena.

14

Around the perimeter lay the control complex hidden beneath its protective covering.

The spacecraft was approaching along a thirty degree ramp, its massive bulk supported on three white-hot pillars of fire. From the tear in its undersurface a jet of fuel sprayed astern. As the craft skimmed over the rim and into the bowl-shaped launch area, the surface beneath it glistened wet. There was a flash followed by a muted explosion and the rear of the craft was enveloped in thick black billowing smoke. The nose of the craft swung round as it sank towards the ground and then it hit. There was a volley of four reports as charges detonated across the launch area, flooding the region with a blanket of an inert gas. The spacecraft disappeared into a dense grey cloud.

3

The White Knight entered the room. The pilot's hands were still being bandaged; his pressure suit had been cut and carefully peeled away to the elbows.

'Richard. You did a fine job. Your passengers are all alive and responding to treatment. Those who are able send their thanks.' His gaze rested on the bound hands and feet. 'And yourself, what do the doctors say?'

The other shrugged. 'It's too soon to say for sure. They think I'll keep all my fingers. It'll be a while before we know.' He winced as the bandage on his left hand was pinned. 'It really hurts. Nurse, unlace this would you?' He lifted his chin and she loosened the ties down the front of the suit. He nodded. 'Thanks, that's better.' The orange medallion resting on his chest flashed in the sunlight.

'Can you tell me what happened?'

He frowned. 'We almost didn't make it. The rebels had seized the spaceport and parts of the capital but were under siege and giving ground. There wasn't much time. Most of our people had boarded, along with some of the wounded and their families, when Straker's Fifth Fleet appeared in Mars-orbit. We tracked their approach; I had to wait until the last second. They opened fire before we expected; they've improved their long-range weapons. The first volley was poorly aimed, didn't do much damage to us, mainly hit the residential area off to the east. By the time I'd powered-up the engines we were in the thick of it. There must have been ten to fifteen beams targeted on the spaceport. Those who weren't already on board were dead. We got into the air. One of the fuel depots went up with us almost on top of it. That was the worst.' He paused. 'A couple of shields failed – they shot us up pretty bad before we got clear. We were still suborbital when we jumped. You know the rest.'

The White Knight laid his hand lightly on his shoulder. 'You did well.'

'How many did I get out?'

'A hundred and thirty-two.'

He sighed, 'So few . . .' He stared, half shook his head. 'Sometimes I think . . .' He caught the other's gaze and shrugged helplessly. 'I don't know what I think. What are we doing? What's the point? We never fight back.' His tone was bitter and frustrated. 'There are thousands dead back there. And then there'll be reprisals. What was it the last time – ten for every one of the Empire's losses? That was Straker too.'

One of the doctors looked across to the White Knight and indicated the door with his eyes. 'Please . . .'

'I'm all right,' the patient objected, 'I just feel sick.'

The old man nodded. 'I must go; the others are waiting to hear.' And then to the doctor, 'I'll come back later when you're finished.' He turned and left the room.

Two men were waiting in the corridor outside. One of them spoke, 'Sir, if we may . . . just one moment?'

'Yes, what is it?'

The other continued, 'My name is Miguel Lopez; I am from the computing center. This is my assistant,' indicating his companion. 'He has found something which we think is very important.'

The White Knight addressed the second man. 'Something important? Concerning the computer?'

'Yes, sir. It is my duty to check the log at the end of each shift. It tells us what jobs the computer has done in the past eight hours. Helps us to keep track of things.'

'I understand.'

'Today, I found an entry which is highly irregular; information drawn from the computer memory banks but apparently without a user identity being given. It's as if no one asked it and it just did it of its own accord.'

The old man frowned. 'I can see that is perplexing; but why come to me over a computer malfunction?'

The other took up the conversation. 'Sir, he came to me as his immediate superior. The importance of the problem lies in the area of memory that was read. Those files were restricted. We identified the terminal to which the information was fed.'

'And?'

'We found this.' He held up a polythene bag containing a printed circuit board. 'It is the board that requests the user's identity code and decides on the basis of the answer it receives what level of access will be permitted.' He indicated one edge. 'Along here, the connections are made to the rack housing the boards. This track here,' he pointed, '. . . you can see has peeled back and been bent sideways so as to contact its neighbor. This must have happened when it was last inserted into the rack. It cannot function in this condition. The last time our technician removed this board was at its six-monthly overhaul two months ago. It was checked and has worked perfectly ever since. The damage could not have been done then.' He paused. 'There is only one possible explanation. Someone

17

else has removed this board. They did so in order to perform some substitution which then enabled them to gain access to the restricted files without alerting the security systems. When they replaced the board, they unknowingly caused the damage we found. It is an act of espionage.'

There was a short silence. The old man's eyes flicked from one to the other. 'How sure are you of all this – everything you've told me?'

'The evidence is clear,' Miguel Lopez replied calmly. 'We are absolutely certain.'

'Who else have you told?'

'No one; we came straight to you.'

'Good. No one else must know of this.' He looked at his watch. 'I have ten minutes before I meet with the Inner Circle of Knights. You must tell me all I need to know before then. Come with me to my quarters.'

4

Five men were seated at the conference table, two on one side, three on the other. Each wore the long, white ceremonial gown of a Knight of the Church. On the breast of each lay a colored, gold-rimmed medallion suspended from the neck by a fine golden chain. On the wall behind the place of honor at the head of the table hung a shining shield. Its diameter was the height of a man. On its surface was richly emblazoned the image of a figure on horseback. His steed was purest white as was the robe in which the rider was clad, save for the fringe dipped in red. On his head he wore a jewelled crown of gold. Around the rim of the shield were the words 'Faithful and True' and the titles 'King of Kings and Lord of Lords.' Beneath the shield were the words 'In His Strength We Stand.'

The doors to the conference chamber opened and a sixth man entered, similarly attired. The others rose as he came into the room. He stood at the head of the table.

'Fellow Knights, let each of us now draw near in silence to the one whom we serve and thank Him for safely returning to us our brother Richard. . . .' Then, after a while, 'Please be seated.'

'The Orange Knight cannot be with us; his wounds are still being tended.' Seeing their alarm, he continued, 'His condition is not serious. I am sure he will make a speedy and complete recovery. He managed to evacuate one hundred and thirty-two refugees: mainly our own people but also several wounded and the families of those involved in the fighting. As we expected, the rebellion was crushed, with the loss of many lives. There was no opportunity for surrender. The Fifth Fleet under Admiral Straker devastated the entire area. The enemy's long-range weaponry has apparently been improved; our technical division will be given a detailed report as soon as possible.'

He paused and one of the others interjected, 'We watched the landing on the closed-circuit TV. What is the state of the spacecraft?'

'Unfortunately, most of it is scattered fairly widely across the launch pad; the leaking fuel was ignited by the reflected exhaust of the thrusters as he prepared to touch down. There is not much that we can salvage. The replacement, Charger 34, has already been under construction for some time, but completion will take several months. Until then Richard will have to be grounded.'

'Do we know how many were killed in the fighting?' another asked.

The White Knight shook his head. 'We can only guess. Maybe five thousand. The Empire is claiming more than ten thousand rebels dead for the loss of eighty-seven of their own men.'

'Have the reprisals been announced?'

'Not yet, but the last time Admiral Straker was involved, the price was put at ten for one. We cannot expect any lower.'

There was a stunned silence. Any sense of victory they might have felt at the success of their rescue mission was crushed beneath the feeling of powerlessness that now overwhelmed them. The hostages would already have been taken prisoner, beginning with the known families of those dead insurgents whose bodies could be identified. The rest of the numbers would be collected at random from the civilian population.

This was the fear by which the Empire ruled. Even to live where a rebellion had taken place was to risk death. No evidence of participation was required. Through fear of this reprisal, many uprisings had been crushed before they even happened. Someone afraid for his life or his family would denounce his neighbor, his friend, his workmate, and would receive from the authorities in recognition of his faithfulness a state pension, extra food allowances and promotion – after of course being resettled anywhere in the Empire he might choose, where the way in which these privileges had been gained would not be known.

Those named would disappear, taken from their beds in night raids. Parents would be taken together for interrogation, to encourage confession. Then they would be separated and sent to the slave factories where they would spend the rest of their useful lives. Eventually they would be abandoned to a slow death in the badlands created by the Great War through which the Empire had come to power. Children, where young enough, would be taken into institutions. Over the years they would be re-educated. Memories of their parents would become dim. The boys would be trained in the military academies for service in the armed forces, the girls for domestic service.

A pretty one might become the personal slave of someone high in authority whom the Empire wished to reward.

'God have mercy on their souls,' someone breathed. The silence lengthened.

'Fellow Knights, we have a second matter to discuss.' The old man could not disguise the sadness in his voice. He regarded each of his friends in turn. 'Brothers, even before the last is over, a new trial is upon us, and one that strikes closer to the heart than any we have faced so far. I have just been informed of an event which has the direst of consequences for all of us. Gentlemen, there appears to be within our city a traitor to our cause, one whose sympathies lie with the enemy.'

There were startled exclamations around the table.

'Someone has penetrated the security systems guarding the computer complex and gained access to our deepest secrets. We must assume that he or she intends to pass on the information to the Empire.'

'But that's impossible!' It was the Blue Knight who spoke. 'The finest minds alive designed and built those systems; they're foolproof.'

'I have evidence to the contrary.'

'What evidence; what's happened?'

'I have just been given a full and detailed report by one of our senior technical staff. The one thing we can be sure of is that a leak of information has occurred.'

'Well?' It was the Magenta Knight. 'You still haven't told us exactly what has happened. Just how serious is this?'

'In brief,' the White Knight continued, 'A circuit forming a critical part of the security system guarding one of the terminals was substituted by a device which enabled the traitor to gain access to restricted information without having the authority to do so and without raising the alarm. However, there were gaps in his or her knowledge and we were able to detect the leak, though several hours after it occurred. We know precisely what information was taken from the computer. They were biographies of all the Church officials on Titan. As well as containing a brief life history, they fully detail our involvement in establishing and sustaining the Church there.

'If this list is transmitted to the security forces of the Empire, all those named will be taken prisoner and interrogated. It would take only a few to yield and more of our people would be discovered. The process could not be halted. In a matter of hours, the Church as a whole on Titan would cease to exist and our position elsewhere throughout the Empire would be severely weakened.'

'How long ago did this happen? You said several hours – how do we know it isn't already too late?'

'It is true that some hours have elapsed since the information was obtained, but in that time the shield surrounding Ekklesia has only been lowered once to allow the Orange Knight to return. During that brief time, there was no outgoing transmission from the surface. Both the traitor and the information he holds are still on Ekklesia.'

'We must take steps immediately.'

'All craft must be grounded; the shield must not be lowered.'

'The traitor obviously has technical skills. We should begin searching with data scanners in the computer staff quarters.'

'We are all agreed on these measures?' The others nodded. 'I shall give the orders myself. No other word of this must go beyond this room. As yet the traitor does not know he has been discovered; it may be that he will give himself away by trying again.'

'There is no guarantee that he will have the disks close at hand; he may have secreted them anywhere on Ekklesia.' It was the Grey Knight who spoke. 'If we don't find them, we can't ground all Charger ships indefinitely; our services will doubtless be required all too soon. What then?'

'It is true, these are only temporary measures. I have given this some thought, and there seems to me to be only one permanent solution. I seek your approval. We must mount a rescue mission to evacuate all those who are named, together with their families. This will mean sending someone to Titan with a copy of the list and a message of explanation from us. Only when we have brought our people to safety here will the information be useless to the authorities and our position secure.'

'I agree; we have no choice in the matter.'

'I agree also.'

'And I.'

'We are unanimous?' They nodded their assent. 'Then we shall reconvene in three hours' time to plan in detail. Do any of you not wish to be considered?' Silence. 'Then, gentlemen, spend the intervening time wisely. We decide in three hours.'

The door slid closed behind the man who had just entered his apartment. The Violet Knight turned to face the newcomer. His expression communicated to the other that all was not well.

'Is something the matter?'

The Knight's tone was scathing. 'Fool! You weren't as clever as you thought. They're on to you.'

'But how?'

'I haven't got time for details, and neither have you. Have you copied the disk?' The young man reached into his pocket and handed it over. His superior continued, 'All craft are to be grounded. In a few minutes' time they will be under a heavy guard. You must work quickly. Before you can leave Ekklesia, you will need to sabotage the shielding device. You know where the control room

23

is? Good. You must take a short-range reconnaissance craft and transmit as soon as you are clear. In addition to the information on the disk, warn the authorities that a rescue is being planned. It may be that for the first time they will capture a Knight alive. Do you understand what you have to do?'

'I understand, but . . .' he paused, 'if I am flying a reconnaissance vehicle, then I will not be able to avoid capture. I will be brought back here and tried as a traitor. You promised me. . . .'

'Anything that was promised you depends on you doing your job successfully. If you manage to transmit the information, I will know. When I leave this accursed planet I will find a way to bring you and your family with me. You will have all that you asked for. Now, we are wasting time, of which we have precious little. Go, and do quickly what you must do.'

His subordinate left. He travelled directly to the spaceport complex. Guards were not yet in position. He reached the defense and communications center, his technician's uniform raising him beyond suspicion. The shift supervisor turned to face him as he entered the shield control room, his face registering surprise as he saw the weapon pointed in his direction. He reached for the alarm.

'Don't touch that!' the other shouted and then fired. A thin blue beam pierced his tunic and his hand slid away from the red button as he sank to the floor, coughing blood.

The other regarded him with disdain, 'Everybody wants to be a hero around here.' Moments later he left the room, closing the door behind him. Inside, the shield control console was a wreck of splintered circuit boards. His victim lay at the center of a steadily widening pool of blood.

6

In the conference chamber, the same five Knights were seated. As before, the White Knight entered and they rose. He took his place at the head of the table and regarded them sternly.

'Gentlemen, be still and know in whose presence you stand, the one who sees all things and from whom no secret is hidden, who searches us and discerns our thoughts and knows our hearts. Now, be seated.'

'Since we last met there have been certain developments. Within minutes of the close of our meeting, the shield had been temporarily disabled and its operator severely wounded. A reconnaissance craft was stolen in an attempt to transmit the information to our enemies, an attempt which very nearly succeeded.' His piercing gaze fell on each of his companions in turn. 'One of you knows what he has done. One of you has betrayed us!'

The double doors flew open and a squad of guards filed into the room. The men at the table, some transfixed in their chairs, others half-risen, found themselves surrounded. The White Knight rose. His whole frame trembled, but when he spoke his voice was devoid of all emotion.

'One of you . . . one of you will answer to God for this.'

7

The old man stood alone in the darkness of the chapel, staring out beyond the silhouette of the cross to the stars beyond. They were beautiful, and he was tired. His thoughts seemed to drift among them. Seventeen years ago he had begun this alone and now he felt alone again. He corrected himself; his son stood with him. Only two were on the Lord's side. His grief had moved him to tears and he struggled to maintain his composure. His heart was heavy, he had taken all the blame on himself. How pitiful was their love for the one who had given all. How small and weak.

He sighed. No words could convey the sadness to his Father.

'Where will this end?' He spoke into the darkness, and again, 'Where . . . ?' he whispered. He stood in the stillness, and wondered. After some moments he seemed to rouse himself, to return to the present and what he was going to do. He left the room and passed through into his apartment and spoke into an intercom.

'Bring the Grey Knight to me.'

He waited. Presently, there was a knock at the door which then opened. He addressed the guard.

'You may wait outside.' The door closed and the one who had been admitted crossed the room. The old man hugged him. 'My son.'

'Father, what's happening?' They regarded one another.

The old man spoke quietly, 'All we have fought for hangs in the balance. You are my named successor and on you depends everything now.'

'Can there really be a traitor within the Inner Circle?' His tone was incredulous.

'I have also been asking that question,' his father replied, 'I cannot believe that it has always been so. We have all risked our lives so many times. And yet now, now someone has turned against us. Why we cannot say, but it must be so. I did not tell all that I knew at the second meeting. The traitor was only partly unsuccessful in his attempt to pass on the information he had obtained. It is true that he had not managed to transmit the data on the disk in his possession, but he did have time to send off a warning of our rescue plan to Titan. That was only known to those of us present at the first meeting. Therefore, one of us must have told him. This was a possibility I had not considered, otherwise I would have been more careful.'

'What can we do now?'

His father shrugged his shoulders. 'We must go ahead with the rescue. Who knows how many are involved in this treachery? If we did nothing, then as soon as we resumed normal operations we would be risking the lives of our friends on Titan. At any time the information denouncing them might be passed to the authorities. We who are sworn to defend the Church would be the cause of its destruction on Titan.'

'But, father, you said the authorities have been alerted to our intentions; how could we possibly manage even to get to Titan undetected?'

'You are right. For us it would be impossible; but there is another way.' He picked up a file lying open on his desk and regarded the photograph on its title page. 'We need the help of an old friend.' He handed the picture to his son.

'The Crimson Knight? I thought he was . . .'

'No, not dead. He escaped the destruction of Diakos, together with his child, Mark. His wife, Natasha, was taken by the authorities. We have not been able to trace her since, but we know that he is still alive. He has taken the name Trentam, Paul Trentam; he works as a geologist for the Corporation. You must go to him.

'Since the loss of his wife he has built a new life for himself and his son on Earth. In order to help us he will have to leave all that behind. And yet I am certain he will do it. One of those named on the list is Isaac. He is old now, but many years ago he and Paul were closer than father and son.'

'How will he get to Titan and then to Ekklesia? Only our own craft are programmed with these coordinates.'

His father handed him a data disk. 'I have prepared this. It contains the list of names our friend will require and a message to the Church on Titan. In addition, it contains the coordinates of Ekklesia; he will be able to use it to program a Corporation ship to bring them here. He must convince his employers to send him to Titan. He must also contact the Church there beforehand. Several of our people are employed by the Corporation; he must convey to them the importance of the information on this disk. He may need their help in keeping it from the authorities.'

The other's eyes were wide with consternation, 'Father, we are risking everything; the location of Ekklesia has never before been written down. It is known only to you. If the Empire obtains this disk our time would be over. If Ekklesia were taken, all our secrets would be laid bare. The whole Church would be plunged into darkness. There would be a terrible slaughter.'

As he talked his father's eyes seemed to stare into space. Now he returned his gaze and replied in a tone of voice that was laden with heaviness.

'Philip, don't you think I have considered these things? This is why I am sending you, and to Paul. You are the two I have chosen as trustworthy. I have sought the Lord in prayer and he has shown me no other way.' There was a long silence.

'Then I'm ready, father.'

The White Knight regarded his son with a father's pride. He handed him several documents.

'Study these carefully; they will tell you where to find our friend. And now . . .' he made the sign of the cross, 'go with my blessing, and may God protect you and bring you back safely to me.'

8

It was dusk; the shadows were lengthening, the air was warm and the night chorus was awakening across the rich green countryside. Swifts darted low over a lazy river, swinging from bank to bank, dipping down to the mirrored surface of the waters and then soaring high among the branches at the riverside, weaving in and out and around in their evening dance.

Two men came into view around a bend in the path that wound between fields and river. They walked slowly, with a relaxed and peaceful air. Both were being soothed anew by the landscape's pleasant charm. The younger was talking quietly, gazing around, reminiscing, drinking in the feel of the evening. His friend, older and fair-haired, listened and nodded sympathetically. They strolled side by side.

'It's so lovely here in the summer.' He sighed. 'I do miss it, Paul; it's so seldom I can come here now. Life in Ekklesia is a different world. We love it, but this was our home.'

Their pace slowed as they came close to the river, and he took in the birds, the reflections in the water, the gentle sway of the trees. He glanced at his companion and smiled.

'In other circumstances I would be glad to be here.' They walked on. He shook his head, 'A lot has happened since I saw you last. We've done some good, but at a price.' His gaze fell and his voice faded a little. 'There are only seven of us now; we used to be twenty. These are hard times, Paul; you wouldn't think it to look around here. If only things had turned out differently.'

'You can't re-write history, Philip. What's past is past. We're here and, for better or worse, so is the Empire.'

'You're right,' the other agreed. 'I know I shouldn't think like that, but it's tempting sometimes. We've been under terrible pressure, and now this; it couldn't have come at a worse time.'

Ahead, the way lay between two gently rising slopes; beyond, the ground became uneven until the path they were following petered out into a number of faint indistinct trails before finally losing itself entirely. They came to a halt and stood in silence. Both wanted to prolong the moment, to delay the separation that would follow. The one who had been talking held out his hand to his friend.

'It's time for you to go back, Paul.'

He nodded. 'Yes, Mark will be home soon. We've come a long way.' He took the offered hand. 'I'll see you again soon, Philip.'

'Yes . . .' He sounded a little too certain. He added lamely, 'We're very grateful, Paul.'

'I'm glad you came.'

Their hands parted. Both men stared at the ground. Neither dared to add any more, to give further voice to the thoughts in his mind. The feeling of quiet communion was gone; they were both ill-at-ease.

'Goodbye, then.'

'Yes, goodbye . . . take care.'

The Grey Knight strode on alone up the path. The other watched until his figure passed out of sight around the next bend and then turned back towards the outskirts of the city. As he walked, he saw neither the countryside around him nor the pebbles at his feet. He was deep in thought. The arrival of his friend, as sudden as was his departure, had given him great pleasure and a gladness that he had not felt for many years. But it had not been merely a courtesy call, or even a renewing of a friendship too long left to fade. It was something more – a necessity, something on which his future would turn. The news his friend had brought, and the package he had left in his charge, were both of vital importance, not only to these two, but also to many others whose lives, as yet, were unaffected; people who at this moment were unaware that events were overtaking them that would leave an irrevocable mark on them all.

It had been nine years now; nine years since the horror of Diakos. Nine years since Natasha. . . . He stopped himself, mentally cutting the sentence short as he felt the pain welling up inside him. How many times he'd had to do that – fight to stop himself remembering. Now it was too late; he could see her clearly, in all her wonderful dark beauty, a beauty from within that was so powerful it had almost frightened him. For nine years he had been struggling with its memory. Now, as he had done so many times before, he tore his mind's eye away.

He turned to the problem of how to arrange his journey to Titan. It should not be difficult. He was a geologist; his job was to predict the occurrence of rare metal sources from geophysical data. He would inform the Corporation that re-examination of some old charts led him to believe there might be a sizeable deposit of commercial value on Titan and he needed to make further tests on site. This was partly true; there was an outcrop he'd meant to check up on some time, but he thought it unlikely that it would turn out to be commercially viable. If all went well they could leave the next day; Mark would have to come with him. This was a one-way trip.

9

The power of the twin boosters faded and the Grey Knight eased forwards in his seat, glanced out at the curve of the Earth turning beneath him, and checked his instruments. Altitude 28 kilometers, vector 4.8 kilometers per second on course 72,147 degrees. On the visual display before him, a fine red line marked his trajectory, arcing up and away from the planet he had just left.

Turning to the main computer keyboard, he requested routine scan. The screen blanked for a moment and then changed to a 3D map centered on his present position, on which several flashing points indicated other objects in space around him. He studied it briefly; nothing but debris and several high-orbit satellites, all non-powered, none coming in his direction. It looked as if he had avoided pursuit.

He typed another key and the screen blanked again. He paused for a moment to reflect. The past twelve hours had raced by. His meeting with Paul had brought back old memories of a time when the select band of which he was a member was new-born and strong, when they had first refused to bow beneath the Empire's rule and pledged themselves to the service of a higher authority. Then, his youthful optimism had carried all before it and life was just an adventure with a certain happy ending. The years between had taught him differently. His hope had not failed and his confidence had shifted to safer ground than the passing glory of youth, but he had nevertheless seen and felt pain and sadness. That had played its part in forming his character.

Now they were all facing the greatest test of all, although as yet only a few knew it. Only minutes after he had regained the safety of the air following his parting from Paul, he had blundered into an Empire security patrol and, with no good reason for being in that sector, had been forced to turn tail and run. It had taken all his skills and the limits of his craft's technology to lose them in what had become a running battle over the South American subcontinent.

He closed his eyes and talked to the God to whose service he had sworn his life, sharing his troubled thoughts and thanking Him for his safety so far. His part in the mission was almost over. He had delivered his cargo to his contact on Earth. All that remained was to compute his jump into hyperspace and he would be back on Ekklesia, the planet-city of the Knights of the Church, which he had so recently left.

He directed the computer to calculate his trajectory and awaited the 'Ready' response. Ahead of him a line of light flashed for an instant and then blazed steadily as the sun rose over the world beneath him. He prayed for safety in the jump to light speed and beyond. A last scan ahead to check for a clear flight-path and he would be ready to . . . He stopped. There was something at bottom right on the screen. He increased magnification and peered into the confusing haze of light. He was scanning almost directly into the oncoming rush of the solar wind and the image was obscured, shimmering. But now he could see quite distinctly three points of light breaking away from the disc of the sun, moving rapidly and in tight formation and swinging onto an interception course. Empire Epsilon fighters. They had used the oldest trick in the book, coming at him out of the sun. Now they were closing rapidly and soon they would be too close to his jump flight path and he would be forced to lose them in real space, with nowhere to hide. He must be on their screens and their maneuverability was equal to his own.

33

He locked in the autopilot to computer control and turned to the defense systems console. Like all Charger ships, his craft possessed no weapons; but the technology at his disposal now to protect it was unrivalled throughout the Empire. Yet the jump to light speed was imminent and only limited power could be diverted. A blanket shield, which would make him practically impervious to all assaults, was impossible. He must match each of their weapons separately as and when they used them.

Twin flashes of orange flooded the screen for an instant: neutron shells that would leave his craft intact for search but kill him instantly. An obvious first choice and one he had predicted. Forward antimatter shields were in position; his craft glowed orange as the matter-antimatter collided. His protection against this weapon was absolute, yet the minute change in mass would cost the computer extra time as it adjusted its calculation. His jump would be delayed some fifths of a second. He started as twin green beams struck the cabin window: lasers. Needle-sharp beams played over the surface of the ship, seeking a fault in the mirror shields built into its skin. For a moment the whole outer surface was surrounded by a web of fine, bright spears.

'Ready.' The computer flashed its message onto the screen. He pushed a button on the main console. The ship surged forwards, streaking towards light speed, and vanished into hyperspace.

10

The sun was shining into Mark Trentam's bedroom when he woke. Outside, the city was already busy. He washed and dressed and took down a book from the shelf.

He read, 'Through faith you are shielded by God's power until the coming of the salvation that is ready to be revealed in the last time. In this you greatly rejoice, though now for a little while you may have suffered grief in all kinds of trials. These have come so that your faith – of greater worth than gold, which perishes even though refined by fire – may be proved genuine. . . .'

He thought about it for a while. The word 'trial' stuck in his mind. The previous afternoon, at school, they had been made to watch the public execution of the hostages taken on Mars. Their trial had consisted of the charges being read out and the judgment being pronounced. There had been no defense. Many of them had been little older than himself.

He went downstairs and into the kitchen. His father had already been up awhile. Mark noticed two suitcases standing in the corner.

'Hi, Dad. You're not going just yet, are you?' he asked.

'Not till after breakfast!' his father replied. 'Here, have some of this.'

They sat down. Father and son, they were alike. Paul Trentam was tall, fair-haired and strongly built. His features conveyed a mixed impression of gentleness and strength. His eyes were a striking emerald color and were mainly responsible for his youthful appearance. He was in his middle forties. Mark, at fourteen, was a younger version of the same, although his hair was darker and the green of his eyes flecked with brown. Between mouthfuls of cereal, he probed his father for information: the size, temperature, surface conditions, everything about the place his father was to visit.

'Well, the last time I was there, you couldn't go outside the City dome; the air was still unbreathable. The oxygen seeding is almost up to twenty percent now; most of the methane's been harvested. You wouldn't notice the difference. The dome has been dismantled. Almost a tenth of the surface has been reclaimed and there are two other smaller cities, Gana and Livea – that's the mining-post where I'll be. There are almost five hundred people there, and if my work confirms the wolfram deposits, it'll be a real boom-town five months from now.'

'When are you going to get back?'

'That's hard to say; could be weeks, maybe even a month. This was a really unexpected find. Two days ago I hadn't even noticed it on my charts; it's a well-disguised outcrop. If it's big . . .' He looked across at Mark's crestfallen expression, 'Anyway, that's why I called your school.'

'Oh, Dad, you didn't have to get them to keep a special eye on me. I'll be fine with Aunt Jane here to look after me.'

'That's not what I called for,' his father replied, and Mark noticed his expression no longer said what he had thought it did.

'This time I could be away for quite a long time; it's better that you come with me. I've spoken to the Principal and it's all arranged.'

'What?' His son's face was incredulous.

Paul waved down the coming explosion. 'All right; I know it's a surprise, but spare me the theatricals. It's going to be no vacation for either of us. I've got a lot to do, and it's very important work. I won't have time to supervise you. There's a library in the main City; I'll expect you to do some serious reading to make up for the time you're missing at school.'

Mark nodded vigorously, but this show of obedience could not disguise the fact that a hundred other thoughts than his father's cautioning remarks were passing through his mind. He started to get out of his seat.

'I'd better get my camera.'

'Right now, you eat your breakfast,' his father said. 'We have a long drive to the spaceport and only a couple of hours to get you through the medical checks once we arrive. Lift-off is scheduled for 15:15. Everything packed. We leave in twenty minutes, no later.'

//

The time was 14:55. Mark and his father had boarded the ship a few minutes earlier. It was a class B Explorer, the *New England*, larger than anything he had previously been on, with a two-robot crew of flight engineer and maintenance slave in addition to the main computer systems. They were in the living quarters and preparing for lift-off.

'Remember, Mark, only in this room are we safe from surveillance; company secrets have to be closely guarded and this room is guaranteed bug-free. But you must remember not to mention anything about the Faith elsewhere in the ship, and especially not in front of the robots; their memory banks can be accessed directly by Empire police.'

'Sure, Dad, I know.' Mark was used to secrecy by

now. He had soon learned to keep quiet after a couple of incidents at school.

Paul Trentam leaned over to the intercom and pressed a button. 'Flight engineer, report on count please.'

'T-minus eighteen minutes ten seconds, sir. All systems operational. Weather conditions ideal. Might I suggest you take your pre-lift medications now, sir?'

'Thank you, engineer. You have my authorization for control of the ship until point C in flight, as programmed.'

He sat back and took the cup that had appeared from the service bay to his right. Mark was being offered a similar drink.

'This will help you to cope physiologically with the G-force of lift off Mark. I think yours should be lemonade flavor.'

Minutes later, at 15:15 precisely, the dart-shaped craft accelerated along the runway, tilted sharply upwards and, with the main thrusters on full power, sliced arrow-like through the thinning atmosphere into the velvet blackness above. It hung briefly in Earth orbit to make course corrections and then engaged light-drive and accelerated away and into hyperspace.

Unknown to both Paul and Mark, their departure from Earth had not gone unnoticed. The security forces of the Empire, alerted by the traitor's warning, had been watching and waiting for this very thing. All recent requests for transit to Titan were being sought out and investigated by their extensive intelligence network. The information received from the Corporation on Paul's intended flight, backed up with the knowledge that he had also taken his son on what was supposedly a business trip, had been enough to arouse their interest. They had taken immediate action, but too late.

At the same moment as the ship vanished into nothingness, thousands of miles away, in the city where it had begun its journey, a squad of black-helmeted secret police burst into an empty apartment and spread out, each taking a room, spilling the contents of desks and drawers across the floor, searching behind and beneath the furniture, testing the walls for hidden cavities. Within minutes the search was over. The squad captain spoke into a hand-held communicator.

'There's nothing here except a single Book; they must have the list with them if contact has been made. I suggest you pull them in on arrival on Titan. We were just too late. Nothing else to report.'

With a curt gesture to the others, he ordered them out and then left himself, pausing for a moment at the door to survey the damage. It had been a close thing and this time they had almost caught them. Unfortunately that satisfaction now belonged to someone else.

The opening moves in this most serious game of hide-and-seek had now been played. As yet, the weaker of the two adversaries had managed to remain one step ahead of the tactics of its more powerful opponent. The prize, the precious object that the Empire was seeking so determinedly, was now sitting snugly in a hidden pocket in Paul Trentam's attaché case on its way to Titan.

12

The *New England* came out of hyperdrive into the shadow of the massive bulk of the planet Saturn. From his view-point in the observatory dome, Mark traced its outline, marked by the absence of stars, and then looked into its featureless black disc. It was a hole into which they were steadily falling, drawn in by its intense gravitational field: a potential energy well into whose depths the slightest error might plunge them. A well whose only bottom would be the moment of implosion.

'. . . the valley of the shadow of death . . .' The words came unbidden to his mind. They were flying through the icy darkness cast by this giant planet; below them a whirling maelstrom of methane and acetylene.

'. . . fear no evil; for you are with me . . .' But here, with Earth a speck which he could no longer see, at the limit of the inhabited solar system, a far-flung outpost. Could God really be here too? He stared despondently into the darkness.

'Even here,' a voice was saying. 'This is not new to me, it is my creation and I am here, around you and inside you. Trust me, I have never let you down, nor will I ever leave you. I am able to keep you safe. Always remember that.'

As the boy pondered, the ship was skimming around the globe, using the giant's pull to reduce speed and bring them to a rendezvous with one of its moons. This lay ahead of them as yet, around the sunlit side of the planet, but they were steadily overtaking it.

Mark looked up. Low over the sunlit crescent of Saturn hung a pearl of light, glowing with a diffuse blue-whiteness: Titan, the sun's rays filtering through its newly-woven mantle of air. He turned and left the observatory. It was time to find his father.

Paul Trentam was already in the living quarters as Mark came in. The look on his father's face surprised him.

'What's wrong . . . ?' A finger to his father's lips motioned him to silence. The door slid shut behind him and locked.

'Listen, Mark. We have only twelve minutes before our rendezvous with Titan, and I have something very important to tell you. For the past seven or eight minutes we have been followed by an Empire scout ship.'

'What?' Mark couldn't help interrupting.

'It's not important in itself,' his father went on. 'But what is important is the message that they just sent to customs control on Titan and that I monitored.' He paused. 'Listen, son. I haven't told you all there is to know about this trip, for your own safety. But now I have to tell you something about why I really came to Titan at such short notice. The wolfram deposit is just a cover. It's probably only a scattered, low-grade deposit – nothing the Corporation would consider mining in a hundred years. That was just something for me to be seen to be doing and to give me a chance to do what I really came here for.'

'What do you mean? I thought you said this find was very important and . . .'

His father turned and reached inside his attaché case. 'Listen, Mark. Do you know what this is?' In his hand he held a small grey disk sealed in a permalite case. It could fit snugly into a man's hand.

'Of course I know, Dad. But what's so important about a floppy disk?'

His father placed the cassette on the table. 'The Empire wants this disk or, more specifically, the information it contains. They'll kill to get it if they have to; and right now they suspect me of having it, which you can see I have.'

Mark was frightened. 'You mean they're going to arrest us when we land on Titan? But why? Why have you got something they want so badly, and where did it come from?'

'I can't tell you, Mark. All I can say is that they probably will detain us both when we arrive. But they mustn't find this disk. There is one way we might manage that.'

He reached into Mark's case. 'I brought your pocket logic games along, but I replaced the games disk with a counterfeit 'copy' of the one on the table, written in the same code but containing routine geological data tables.'

As he spoke he uncased the disk on the table, slid it into the pocket games unit, and placed the one he had just removed in the permalite cassette.

'I have altered the controls of your games set so that attempting either to play or to remove the disk will wipe it clean. The only way it can be removed intact now is to disassemble the unit. I'll conceal this counterfeit disk in an inner pocket, where it will be found if they use a data scanner on me. I will tell them the truth – that it's geological data, but encoded for protection of the Corporation's interests. They won't believe me and will either have to apply to headquarters in Livea for translation, which will take time, or – and this is what I think they'll do – try to break the code themselves. At any rate they'll think they've got what they're after and probably won't bother to search you. That might just give us enough time: time for you to make the contact that I can't.'

'But, Dad, I can't go off on my own; I've never been in the City before. I wouldn't know where to go or what to do.'

'I know that,' his father replied. 'But it's not your problem. From the moment we both step onto Titan, friends will be watching our every move. I think we'll be separated. You'll probably be confined to the hotel while I am questioned. Then it's up to them to reach you. In a while, when the authorities have found that the disk is just what I said it is, they will have to let me go. But they are bound to search you and your belongings before they allow me to rejoin you. It's up to our friends to have taken the real disk before that happens. They know every detail of this plan. We discussed it on Earth before we left, although we hoped for your sake that we wouldn't have to risk putting you in danger by using it.'

The intercom flashed an orange light and the flight engineer's metallic tones came to them through the speaker.

'Making final approach now, Mr. Trentam. We are locked into Titan's landing guidance systems and will touch down in approximately one minute twenty seconds.'

'Remember, Mark,' said his father as they strapped in for landing, 'God is with us – with both of us.'

13

The spaceship stood alone at the center of a brightly lit hangar. Through the airlock window Mark watched a small buggy carrying three passengers emerge from the shadows close to the walls and taxi towards them. The outer door swung open as pressure equalized and the hydraulic system lowered the platform on which he and his father were standing gently to the ground. He blinked in the glare of the massed banks of spotlights.

The buggy drew level and two men alighted: the first a blue-uniformed customs official, the second a spaceport guard. Mark's eyes flicked down to the hip holster.

'Mr. Trentam? My name is Johnson, Customs control. If you will accompany me to reception I'm sure we can dispense with the necessary formalities with the minimum of delay. Your Corporation has informed us of the nature of your business and we were expecting your arrival. This won't take a minute – if you please . . .' He indicated the back seat of the vehicle and all four climbed aboard.

'You know, we really are quite excited about this find of . . . wolfram, isn't it? It could mean a lot to the City, and indeed to Titan as a whole.' He spoke over his shoulder.

'Of course,' replied Mark's father. 'If my studies confirm the extent and quality of the ore deposit indicated by my preliminary investigations, the next few years should see a sizeable mining investment in Titan. I'm sure the governing body will be able to channel the extra revenue into making it a very pleasant and prosperous place to live, and our investors will be guaranteed a secure return for the next decade or so. A rare-metal find is good news for everybody.'

'Quite,' replied the administrator as they drew to a halt in the reception bay. He extracted several papers from a file. 'Please check through this and mark off any of the listed items you have in your luggage.'

They crossed to a desk and Johnson sat down. Paul Trentam scanned the list and signed each sheet individually, then handed them back.

'Thank you. If you would step into the scanner . . .' He indicated two vertical posts. Mark's father moved over and stood between them. The official pressed a key on a panel in the desk; after a pause an orange light glowed. Mark noticed that the guard had moved around to a position between them and the exit, and that his hand was resting lightly on the holster at his side. The boy's pulse quickened.

'Ah.' The administrator looked up. 'I see you are carrying some form of data storage disk.' He glanced down, 'I don't think you indicated that here.'

'Oh, of course,' Mark's father replied, reaching into his inside pocket and grinning a little sheepishly. 'I'm sorry, I quite forgot. I have this geological data disk on me.' He withdrew the permalite cassette. 'Just lists correlating ore grades and economic viability, processing costs – that sort of thing. There's much too much to remember in your head.'

The man took the container. 'Quite. I'm afraid we must, of course, verify the nature of the information. We have a disk reader here. Please take a seat; it won't take long.'

'Well, actually it's not that simple, unfortunately,' Mark's father apologized. 'It's a company policy to code all stored data for our protection. If you don't have a Corporation decoder I'm afraid your disk reader won't be able to make heads or tails of it.'

44

The Customs officer looked up sharply. 'Do you have a decoder in your luggage?'

'Oh no. It's strictly a desk unit, much too bulky to be comfortably portable, I'm afraid. The only decoders on Titan, as far as I'm aware, will be in Livea, in the Corporation offices there.'

The official paused, turning the cassette over in his hands. 'Hmm. In that case I'm afraid we must ask you to remain at reception until we can obtain the code specifications from Livea to program our disk readers here. In the meantime we will carry out preliminary tests using our own decoder. I'm afraid all this will take a little time, but that can't be helped. Perhaps your son would like to go on to your hotel with a guide from the City tourist bureau and wait for you there.'

'Certainly,' Mark's father replied. 'That's very good of you. I'm sorry to cause all this trouble.' He turned to Mark. 'Sorry about this, son. I should've remembered I had that disk on me and that they'd want to check it through; data smuggling is big business these days. Still, it shouldn't take more than about . . . half an hour?' He half-turned to the administrator who was speaking quietly into a radiophone handset. The man nodded agreement.

'Here's the account number the Corporation has cleared with the hotel, and my staff credit card. Show them at the reception desk and you shouldn't have any trouble checking in. And don't go wandering off on your own anywhere. Stay in the rooms till I get there.'

'OK, Dad.'

The official turned to the guard behind him. 'Show our young friend the way to the City transport area and wait with him until the guide arrives. Mr. Trentam, we can contact your people from my office, which is also more comfortable.' He rose from his chair.

Paul Trentam leaned down to pick up his attaché case from beside the desk, and as he did so glanced over towards an emergency exit light glowing in the darkness of the hangar perimeter. A point of light blinked on and off twice. He turned and followed the administrator in the direction of the Customs offices.

In the gloom, a black-uniformed figure crouched behind the chassis of a tow truck, speaking softly into a wrist transceiver.

'The boy is leaving – only one guard. Trentam just gave the signal.' He pocketed the pencil-beam flashlight. 'The boy has the disk. Repeat, the boy; they've had to switch. I'm on my way.' He straightened, checked the silver lapel badge which bore the single word 'security,' and backed out through the door behind him.

14

Mark was sitting in a row of padded seats along the wall of a spacious hall. Through the panelled glass doors across the room he watched a steady stream of city buses arrive and depart, ferrying people to and from the spaceport. The guard, sitting casually in the adjacent seat, smoked a cigarette. His eyes drifted over the crowd, then to the digital clock over the entrance. Only twenty minutes till he came off duty. Looking after the kid was a soft job. But if the guide didn't turn up soon he might end up doing some unpaid overtime.

His attention went back to the figures passing by. Then he whipped the cigarette out of his mouth, stubbed it hastily in an ashtray and jumped from his seat as he spotted a black-uniformed figure descending the escalator. As the other approached, he maintained his pose of alert readiness, then saluted precisely and with respect. The two faced one another, identically uniformed in black except for the single white strip on the newcomer's sleeve.

'You are relieved, 27. Make your report to Lieutenant Snider before going off duty. The boy hasn't been out of your sight?'

'No, sir.'

'Spoken to anyone?'

'No, sir.'

'Good. Johnson's certain we've got them this time; they obviously didn't know we were on to them and didn't expect a search. A good day's work. Dismissed, 27.'

'Sir.' The guard turned to leave.

His superior leaned down and lifted the still-smoking butt from the ashtray. 'Oh, corporal . . .' The guard turned. 'You know the rules. Next time be a little more careful. Wouldn't want to start a fire, would we?' He ground the cigarette end firmly into the tray. The guard reddened.

'Yes, sir; I mean no, sir.' He strode off hurriedly.

Mark looked up at his new jailer, who seemed surprisingly young for the authority he had shown in the brief encounter with his subordinate. His expression was impassive, giving no clue to his thoughts. Nothing in his manner accounted for the apprehension the boy was feeling. The uniform itself made him feel afraid. He wished his father were with him. He was alone.

'Help us, Father God, please help us,' he prayed silently.

The man sat down and looked him straight in the eye. 'What's your name, kid?'

'Mark Trentam, sir.'

The man felt in his pocket. 'OK, Mark. See that machine over there?' He pointed.

'Yes, sir.'

'Fetch me a coffee, white no sugar. You want a fruit juice?'

'No thank you, sir.' He took the coins the man was holding out to him.

'OK. Straight there and back; and remember, I can see you all the way.' Mark bent down to his bag.

'That stays here,' the man intervened firmly.

'Yes, sir,' mumbled Mark. He got up and walked over to the machine. He could feel the other's eyes on his back. He brought back the drink, avoiding meeting the man's gaze, sat down and stared at the floor. As each minute went by he was feeling more and more frightened by what was happening. Back in the Customs office they would be programming their decoder with the information supplied by the Corporation in Livea. Soon they would know that the disk they had wasn't the one they were looking for. Then they would be coming for him; and here he was trapped with an armed guard and with no chance of passing the games unit on to his father's contact, even if he knew who he was and where to find him. A new voice made him look up.

'Captain?' His guard rose and took the hand that was offered to him.

'Miss.'

'Tatiana Ivanovna,' she smiled. 'I believe I am to accompany our young friend,' she looked at Mark, 'to the Hotel Imperial and see that he is safely settled in.'

'That is correct, Miss. He has no knowledge of the City whatsoever, and we are very concerned that he should not lose his way,' replied the Captain, stressing the 'very.'

'Indeed?' the woman replied, raising an eyebrow quizzically. 'Well, Captain, you can be assured I shall take very good care of him.' She turned to the boy. 'Hello, Mark. Oh dear, is it really as bad as that?'

Mark stood up quickly. 'No . . . I'm fine thank you.'

She smiled again. 'You really musn't be frightened by the Captain's outward appearance you know; I'm sure he's quite friendly underneath that uniform.' Mark's guard coughed and adjusted his collar. 'Well then, let's go, shall we? Captain, if you wouldn't mind . . .'

'Ahem, no, not at all.' He picked up the case and they crossed the hall and passed through the doors which swung open automatically.

48

Although on the outside Mark was quiet and subdued, inside his mind was a whirl of conflicting thoughts and emotions. There had been too many surprising events in the last few hours, and the arrival of his guide had been the last and most unexpected of all. Here, on a planet millions of miles from home on Earth, he had met a woman he had known all his life.

15

In a locked cubicle in the men's locker room the Captain took a small tool from an inside pocket and reached up to a ventilator grille, inserted the blade between it and the wall, and worked his way around, loosening the frame and prizing it free. This he placed carefully on the floor, propped up against the door. Then he reached into the shaft, withdrew a black plastic bag and emptied its contents: a grey pullover, trousers and cream jacket, onto a shelf.

With unhurried, deliberate actions he removed his black uniform and changed into the civilian clothes, stowing the Captain's garments in the bag after first removing the 'security' insignia. This he placed on the shelf next to the small plastic box he had removed from Mark's bag. Finally he replaced the air duct cover, pocketed the badge and games unit, and blew away the faint traces of plaster that had come away with the grille as he pried it loose.

He stood silent for a moment, until he was sure there was no one in the outer locker room. Then he unlocked the door and stepped out, walked over to the towel incinerator unit, deposited the black bag in it and pressed the 'on' switch. He emerged into the main entrance hall, tossed the metal insignia into a waste disposal unit and strolled out of the building.

'Thank you, Father,' he prayed silently. 'Thank you.'

Lieutenant Snider yawned. He was tired and bored, his office was too warm, and he still had another three reports to read before he could take his meal break. He scanned the sheet in his hand, muttering to himself.

'. . . continued surveillance from moment of arrival . . . yeah . . . remained with the boy until relieved by squad Captain 05 at 14:10. Report filed 14:27.'

'Oh no,' he yawned. He leaned forward, flicked the intercom switch on his desk, and drawled. 'This is Lieutenant Snider. Corporal 27 report to my office immediately – and I mean now.' He slouched back in his chair and waited. Presently there came a knock at the door. 'Yeah'. It opened and a figure in civilian clothing entered and crossed to the desk. Corporal 27 saluted.

'You wanted to see me, sir?'

'Sure did.' The Lieutenant leaned forward and pointed with his pen. 'How long have you been with the spaceport unit, 27?'

'Two months, sir.'

'Two months. And in that time have you managed to count up just how many officers with the rank of Captain we have here?'

'Why . . . uh, yes, sir.' There was a long pause.

'Well?'

'Five, sir.'

'Now isn't that strange. I've been here fourteen years and I only ever counted four.'

The other shifted his weight uneasily. 'Yessir, I mean four, sir.'

'Idiot.' The Lieutenant sighed in exasperation. 'OK, who was it? Fenton, Greenberg, Wallis or Horne?'

Two-seven thought carefully, and as he did so the

50

uneasy feeling in the pit of his stomach grew and grew. Finally he ventured,

'Uh, neither of those, I mean none of those, sir.'

The Lieutenant looked up at his subordinate's paling face and a dawning realization spread across his features. The Corporal swallowed.

'Well, then, who the heck was it?' The question hung in the air, unanswerable. A knock came at the door and Johnson, the Custom's officer, entered.

'Lieutenant, sir, we have just decoded the disk. It is precisely what Trentam described it to be: geological data. What we are after must be on the boy.' He looked from one face to the other. 'Lieutenant? Is something wrong?' Snider slumped back in his chair, closed his eyes and shook his head gently.

'The Commissioner's not going to like this. . . .'

As far back as he could remember, Mark had always had nightmares. He remembered his father coming into his room to wake him as he shouted out in his sleep, and how he would burst into tears and cry in his father's arms, frightened and confused by the images inside his head.

Sometimes he saw a city ablaze, a roaring inferno, and he was running through the streets, glass shattering around him and flames leaping out from doorways. His clothes were torn, his hair singed by the heat, and his eyes stung and watered as he tried to open them in the dense, billowing smoke. Somewhere a voice was calling and he was trying to run towards it. But his way was barred by sheets of flame, piles of rubble. He stumbled and the street burned his hands and knees as he fell. A building in front of him, devoured by the conflagration, swayed, turned and toppled towards him, a crumbling avalanche of glass, steel and concrete. . . .

Another time he was in a room, seated in a chair, unable to rise, hardly able to turn his head. A small, thin man was leaning over him, peering into his eyes with a bright light. In his ears were strange, meaningless noises. A voice was asking him questions. He must answer. He

51

must, or the pain would come again – and then flashing lights, sickening colors, inhuman sounds and horrible twisted creatures were reaching out for him, clawing at his arms and legs.

'Dad, Dad . . .' Somewhere there was a woman's voice and wretched, heaving sobbing.

'No, please, no . . . please, he doesn't know anything, please stop . . . oh God, help us, please help us . . .'

Again, sometimes he was crying, held tightly by some-one who was crying too; and then strong arms took him and pulled him away. It was his father, lifting him and carrying him off. He didn't understand that he must stay. He gazed back over his shoulder to where the woman lay reaching out to him, and then her head dropped and she covered her face with her hands.

'No, Dad, no!' He was crying, pummelling his father with his fists. 'Please, Dad, don't take me away . . .' But now he could no longer see her, and his father was run-ning, and it was very, very dark.

Now Mark relived all these dreams. He could remem-ber them all in vivid detail and as he did so he became more and more convinced that the woman in his dreams was the woman sitting next to him. Everything about them was identical: the way they looked, the way they spoke and the way they moved. This voice was the one that called to him as he ran through the streets. These eyes were the ones that had filled with tears as his father dragged him away. These hands were the ones that had hung on to him for long moments in the last goodbye. He wanted to pull her sleeve and say, 'It was you, wasn't it? It was.' He wanted this stranger to look at him the way the woman of his dreams did, and to hold him, and . . . to love him.

Mark could remember nothing of his mother. She had been killed in a car accident when he was very young. All he knew about her was what his father had told him over the years; that she was very beautiful, thought of others before herself, and gave to the Lord a life of quiet courage.

Mark did not understand why he could remember

nothing about her at all; it seemed to him there should be something. Neither did he understand why he had the dreams, nor who the woman was who filled them. His father had been able to give him no explanation. Yet he was sure that somehow they were all part of the same story; that if only he could understand about one of them, the rest would become clear too.

The bus continued on its journey to the hotel. He did not even notice the City passing by. He looked across at the woman beside him. Why didn't she recognize him? She was acting as if she really had never seen him before in her life. But she must have; he couldn't be wrong, could he? Words came into his mind, words he had read in his Book only days before.

'If any of you lacks wisdom, let him ask God who gives to all men generously and without reproaching, and it will be given him.'

'Please, Father God,' he thought, 'please help me to understand these things, and who the woman is. I want to know very much. I want to know about my mother.'

A wall panel slid back and the two men entered. They found themselves in a room without windows, dark except for a pool of light at its center, from a source hanging low over a large circular table. As they paused, the door slid silently shut behind them and twin spotlights faded up to illuminate their faces.

'Ah, gentlemen . . . How good of you to join me so promptly. Please be seated.'

Snider and Johnson exchanged apprehensive glances and stepped forward to the table. Two chairs rose from the floor to accommodate them and the spotlights followed their steps, continuing to bathe them in a harsh white light.

'I do not believe you have met Commander Lensky. I have personally placed him in complete control of this operation.'

To the left around the table they now noticed another figure in the black uniform of the Empire security forces. Only the hands, clasped immobile on the table top, were clearly visible. The rest of the figure merged with the darkness surrounding him.

'And so, gentlemen – to business.' The two men turned to face the direction from which the voice was emanating. Again the low light left the figure enveloped in gloom and they focussed on the hands, black-gloved, which now took up a document from the table.

'I have here your reports, from which I understand that the information we seek is still not in our hands, although it was, until recently, shall we say – within our grasp?'

'Quite so, Commissioner. . . . They were,' Johnson coughed, 'uncommonly ingenious.'

'So I see.' There was a long silence during which Snider nervously rubbed his neck inside his collar.

'Gentlemen. You were fully aware of the vital nature of this information in our struggle against these criminals. It will enable us to deal a crushing blow and take us one step closer to their utter destruction!' A black clenched fist struck the table. 'Your arrest has been ordered by the Chief Commissar himself. However, I am not so lenient. You have failed in your duty to the Empire and to me, there is only one possible penalty.'

So saying, out of sight beneath the table a button was depressed. Semicircular bolts sprang from the body of each chair around the waist of the occupant, and the two

54

seats began to sink back silently into the floor from which they had risen.

'No, please no, Commissioner . . .' The two men struggled to free themselves, their heads disappearing below the table top. 'No, you can't . . .' The floor slid back over the space into which the two bodies had been drawn.

The third figure shifted uneasily.

'Commander! You appear to be uncomfortable in your seat?' The voice dropped a tone and hardened. 'Do not fail me, Commander Lensky; I am – I believe the expression is – "a bad loser".'

Mark and his escort were seated in a third-floor room in the suite reserved for his father in Hotel Imperial. His guide was describing the sights of the City in a confident, sing-song voice. She did not appear to be talking to him in particular, but rather to the room as a whole. Mark was content to watch her gestures and listen to the sound of her voice. He had forgotten about the disk which, as far as he knew, was still in his bag. For the moment his companion was commanding all his attention. Vague notions, attempts at explanations, passed through his mind. One of these, which at the time seemed no more important or close to the truth than the rest, was that something wasn't right. It was only the dimmest awareness, and he got no further with it and passed on to other things. He was interrupted as she broke off in mid-sentence.

'Oh, I see I'm talking too much,' she smiled. 'Excuse me for a moment, won't you?' She rose and walked into the bathroom, closing the door behind her.

Mark went over to the window. Three floors below, the City was busy with traffic at the end of the day, although this day and night was entirely of man's making. This far out, the sun's light was too weak to provide much variation, or indeed any light at all. Here in the City the daytime brightness was provided by 'Sun City,' an orbiting engineering complex twenty kilometers overhead, converting fusion power into a beam of light energy aimed down through the atmosphere to the surface below, illuminating an area of one hundred square kilometers and establishing the cycle of night and day as the power of the beam waxed and waned with a twenty-four-hour period. Evening was rapidly approaching.

In the bathroom, Tatiana Ivanovna was standing with her wristwatch held to her ear, listening intently to a small, clear voice. It was the voice of Commander Lensky.

'We must assume they now have the disk. Their agent was alone with the boy for several minutes before your arrival. Our only leads now are the boy and his father. We must follow their every move and wait for them to contact the Church again. And they must be kept apart to double our chances.

'The father will be released shortly, but not before a patrol has been despatched to bring in the boy. If his friends are monitoring you both, that might force them into trying to snatch him. On no account are you to be separated. Those are your instructions.'

She pressed a button on the rim of the watch and the crystal display returned to hours and minutes: 16:35. She paused for a while to consider. For the moment it was better that her true allegiance remain hidden. Then, whether the Church made a move or not, she would remain safe. She knew enough of both sides to realize whom to fear the most.

She was standing in front of a wall mirror. Now she looked into her own eyes. The image seemed flat and showed only the surface. Behind that reflection was someone playing a role, or, to be more exact, a role within a role. As far as Tatiana Ivanovna was concerned, nothing was what it seemed to be, nor had it been for a very long time. She tidied her hair, smoothed down the grey jacket and unlocked the door.

Unseen by either of them, in the adjacent suite a figure was seated by the window, listening over a similar wrist transceiver to the conversation next door, relayed via a small microphone taped to the underside of the table. So it was that he clearly heard Tatiana Ivanovna's exclamation of surprise as she spotted the security patrol pull up to the hotel in the street below.

The man jumped to his feet, pulled back the curtain for an instant, then crossed the room at a run, switching off the wrist-receiver as he moved. He burst into the corridor and entered the next room.

'Mark! You have to come with me.' All three froze as the man recognized Mark's guide, she recognized him as the man who had posed as a Captain, and Mark struggled to make some sense of it all.

'Come on, boy – that squad's after you. They'll be here in a minute . . .'

Mark, unable to understand what was happening, clung to the one thing he felt he could trust.

'No, I'm not going. I'm staying with her.' And he literally grabbed hold of the woman's sleeve.

'What? What's all this?' she exclaimed. Surely he couldn't remember? He had been so young.

'Oh no!' His would-be rescuer groaned. 'Look, I don't know why you've taken such a liking to her, but I'm telling you she's probably one of their people. Didn't your father explain? You've got to come with me.'

'No, I won't.' Mark dug in his heels. He would not admit the possibility that he had been betrayed by the woman who had called to him for so many years. The 'Captain' paused, his mind racing.

'All right, she comes too. It's safer to keep her from giving a description of me anyway, until we're out of the City.' He turned to her, 'Are you coming willingly, or do I have to carry you?'

Tatiana looked from him to the boy and back to him. She didn't want to appear too willing, but they must be certain of getting away.

'All right, all right.'

They spilled out into the corridor, the man locking the door from inside and then pulling it shut behind him. Then they ran to the far end and into the fire exit stairwell. As the swinging doors came to rest behind them, the leading squad member reached the top of the main staircase, two others burst from the elevator and they converged on the room so recently vacated.

The squad Captain pressed the muzzle of his laser gun against the doorjamb, slid it past the lock, and the door swung open into the empty room. After a brief search, he spoke into his communicator, and there was a grin of satisfaction on his face.

'They're gone, Commander Lensky; and they've taken agent Ivanovna. She can lead us straight to them.'

17

'Jonathan! Thank God you are safe . . . and you have the boy!' The old man had been pacing back and forth by the fire, and he came over and clasped Jonathan – for that was the 'Captain's' name – by the shoulders, smiling broadly. Tatiana stepped in through the doorway. 'And what is this? We have another guest! And much more agreeable than your ugly self too! Irène,' he called, 'bring food and water. I'm sure you must be hungry.' He beamed from one to the other. 'Please, sit down, sit down. Tell me, Jonathan – did everything go well? Do we have the package, that . . . what is it called . . . disk?'

'Yes, father,' came the reply. 'It is safe. I have it with me. But it is not safe to talk in front of this woman; I found this wrist transceiver on her.' He placed the watch on the table. 'She is almost certainly an Empire agent.'

'Oh, Jonathan,' the old man chided. 'You always were one for melodrama! She is such a slight young thing, how could she possibly bear us ill?'

The son shook his head. 'Father, you are too trusting, too ready to see the good in people, and too slow to see the bad. Please believe me and speak with care.'

'Mmm,' the old man nodded thoughtfully. Then he turned to Mark, his features breaking into a smile once more. 'So you are Mark. Ah, you are just like your father, a fine boy, fine boy.' He patted Mark's hand. 'I remember when your father, my very dear friend Paul, was not much older than you are now. Yes indeed . . .' He shook his head, lost in reverie. 'I too was younger then . . . younger and stronger.'

Mark stared at the old man. 'You know my father?'

'Know him?' he laughed happily. 'My dear boy, we travelled half the solar system together; and those were the days before this umm . . .' He searched for the word.

'Hyperdrive,' Jonathan interjected.

'Yes, hyperdrive. Ah, yes, I knew him well and it has been so long now, so long: fourteen years – or is it fifteen? I forget.' He regarded Mark with a kindly gaze. 'You mean he never mentioned old Isaac to you? Of course, I wasn't so old in those days. Well, well . . . you know, he always could keep a secret.' He fell silent again.

Mark was bursting with questions. How was it that there seemed to be so many people on this planet to do with his father's past and his own? Who was this gentle old man with his flowing grey beard and his clear grey eyes, who spoke so warmly of his father?

'I wish someone would tell me what this is all about!' he exclaimed in exasperation. 'And where I am, and what I'm doing here, and how you know so much about my father, and . . .' Old Isaac laughed and waved down his questions.

'So you've found your tongue at last have you? Well, you shouldn't take too much notice of me, you know. Sometimes I talk and talk and talk. The important thing now is to eat and drink and make you feel at home! When your father arrives we can tell old stories and remember times past . . . fifteen years. The Lord has done a lot for me since I last saw your father; and for him, no doubt, and maybe even for you. "His goodness is from generation to generation." But now,' he rose from his chair, 'let us see if we can find some fruit or something. Where is my wife? She knows where everything is . . .' He ambled into the kitchen.

Paul Trentam had been released by the authorities. He had gone straight to the hotel and found that Mark had disappeared. Presumably he was safe with Isaac and Jonathan. He knew that the time for pretense was now over.

He was sitting in a street bar drinking coffee. Seated at a table behind him, he knew, was a tall heavyset man in a dark gray suit, reading a daily paper. From the moment he left the spaceport, he had known he was being followed; instinct and years of training had not been totally dulled over his fifteen-year respite.

The question now was how to get rid of him before he made contact with the Church. He felt uneasy. It was so long since he had played these games and he had lost some of his youthful confidence. It seemed strange to be relearning the old tricks, sharpening the senses again. And he knew that he had to get everything right first time. Second chances just didn't exist. Still, he tried to reassure himself, God was the same, and just as able to save him now as in those other, younger days.

He paid his bill and stepped out onto the pavement. It was the height of the rush-hour now, and the best chance he was likely to get. A steady stream of traffic passed both ways. He watched carefully. Every fifteen or twenty vehicles was a City transport bus, taller than the individual privately-owned cars. If he could place one of them between himself and his companion he could be lost to view for a moment. That would have to be long enough.

He glanced over his right shoulder as if searching for a break in the traffic. Sure enough there, two or three car-lengths away, was his shadow. He looked away sharply as Paul turned, avoiding eye contact.

Paul Trentam followed the progress of a bus towards him, gauged its speed and glanced in the other direction.

A second bus was approaching. The two would pass one another, he guessed, some half dozen paces to his left.

Suddenly he broke into a run; over his shoulder he saw the bus drawing level. His 'tail' had been caught off-guard and was now several paces further behind, struggling through the crowd. Paul swerved out in front of the oncoming vehicle and made the safety of the middle of the road. The other bus was already level and he was sandwiched in the narrow gap between them, the aluminum wall of the one behind him almost brushing his left elbow. Then the rear of the second bus flashed by. He was still hidden from view by the one behind, and he leapt for the passenger board, landed on one foot, caught hold of the safety rail, and swung his body on to the vehicle. Back down the road, his opponent was searching haplessly in either direction along the street. He was already just another face in the crowd, indistinguishable from all the others.

He turned to find a seat. The conductor regarded him with a patronizing air.

'You know, if you're really that bored with life, there must be an easier way.'

18

Mark was in a small bedroom in Isaac's home, lying down, exhausted, on the bed. It was late evening. His father had still not arrived and, despite Isaac's attempts to distract his attention, he had begun to feel very unhappy. It was bad enough to find himself without his father and in the care of strangers, but what made it worse was being no nearer to finding out what was going on.

Isaac's wife, Irène, had arrived a few minutes after them. She was a small, busy woman. She had to be – just to look after her husband who was more than a little absent-minded. She had rescued the stew she had left him in charge of while she went out, and which he had completely forgotten, and they had all eaten together.

Their meal had been interrupted by a steady stream of visitors, most of whom did not even enter the house. They merely exchanged a few quiet words at the door with the son, Jonathan, and then went their way. Mark could not hear a word of what they said, but he got the impression they were each told the same thing. Some message was being passed on. He supposed it was about the disk which seemed to be at the center of the mystery he was caught up in. Apart from these guarded conversations, Jonathan said little. And the reason, Mark knew, was Tatiana Ivanovna.

Mark felt very frustrated. With her there he knew he would find out nothing about what was happening, except for an odd indiscretion on Isaac's part. Jonathan was careful to change the subject before his father could give too much away.

On the other hand, Mark desperately wanted to talk to Tatiana, to try to find out how she came to be the woman he had dreamed about as far back as he could remember. But he could not ask her such things with the others there. He was too afraid he would make a fool of himself; it all seemed so impossible. Besides, she did not seem in any mood for talking.

In fact, Mark decided, she was acting very strangely altogether. Several times he had looked up from his plate to find her watching him with an expression he couldn't really understand. It was the sort of look he had on his face when he had done something wrong but hadn't yet come round to admitting it. Something was making her sad, something to do with him. But when she saw he had noticed she looked away quickly and gazed fixedly at the table, apparently ignoring him.

He studied her very carefully. Her hair was black, parted in the middle, falling in a gentle wave and then swept back, taken up into a knot. Her eyes, too, were dark, and full of emotions that he felt very strongly but couldn't quite describe.

He thought she was very beautiful. But he saw now that the likeness to the woman in his dreams was not complete. Tatiana Ivanovna was older. That, he realized with a start, was in a way even more remarkable. For the woman he dreamed of was the Tatiana of nine years ago, as she would have looked when he was only five years old. These images came from nine years ago. They had both grown older, while the dream remained unchanged.

Much to his disappointment, as soon as the meal was over she had said she felt a little tired and asked if she might lie down somewhere. Irène had shown her into the guest room, where she had remained for the rest of the evening. Jonathan had left on some business and Isaac had settled down in an armchair by the fire to read his Book and fallen asleep. Irène had tidied away after the meal, with Mark's help, and then taken out a sewing-basket and busied herself with some embroidery.

Mark had come to lie down in the bedroom that he and his father were to share that night, but sleep was far away. He had prayed for his father and then prayed again that he might be able to understand about Tatiana Ivanovna. Then he did in fact fall into a fitful sleep.

As he closed his eyes, the years fell away. He was taken back to another city on another planet, a city empty of people and consumed by raging fires. Again he clung close to a woman whose name he did not know, felt the dampness of her tears on his cheeks and her hand running through his hair.

'Don't cry, please don't cry . . .' he was saying. She held him at arm's length, her eyes drinking in his appearance, casting the memory that must last forever. Her lips trembled, her eyes brimmed with tears. Strong arms took hold of him, their outstretched fingertips clung for a second and then they were torn apart.

'No . . .' he gasped. 'Please, no! . . .' His eyes opened, 'Oh, please God, please . . .' He rushed from the room, flung open the door and ran to the bed where the woman was lying. 'It was you, it was you!' he gasped, and as she turned, he saw the tear-stained cheeks and tear-filled eyes, and felt her arm slip around him and draw him close. Then he could feel her tears on his face as they clung to one another: a boy and his mother's twin sister.

19

Lensky turned from the agent he had just dismissed. Events had taken another turn for the worse. They had lost contact with the father. He tried to keep from thinking of the fate of Snider and Johnson; he must remain calm, cool and objective, if he was to bring this operation to a successful conclusion.

At every stage they had clearly been outwitted by their opponents and he was not going to repeat his predecessors' mistake of underestimating them. But what could he do? The men under his command were the best, known and feared throughout the Empire, products of the most rigorous training program ever devised. And yet they were more than matched by their adversaries.

He paced his office. Until now, he had proceeded along standard lines of investigation that had been tried and tested and proved effective over and over again. Yet to anyone familiar with the methods of the Security forces, he realized, this would render them predictable. This was the weakness that the enemy was exploiting. What he needed was a trump card. The people at his disposal were not enough; he required something more, something unexpected, something unknown.

Isaac woke from his doze and looked across to where his wife sat sewing at the table.

'Irène.' He spoke in a half-whisper. She looked up. 'Irène. The boy, where is he now?'

She smiled. 'Dear Isaac. You were right. He has gone in to talk to her; they are together now.'

The old man carefully closed the book on his lap. 'Good, good. The Lord does indeed work in strange ways.' He smiled. 'You know Irène, there is hope for my memory yet. She did not remember me, but I . . . how could I forget the face of the bride of my closest friend?

'The moment she came in through the door I recognized her. But I don't think she could tell. For some reason she wasn't ready then to confide in the boy or Jonathan. I saw that quite clearly. So I played it up a little; you know how I am. Jonathan was too busy thinking of her deceitfulness to notice mine. When he returns we must explain to him; otherwise he might say something to hurt her without realizing it.'

He leaned over to a bookshelf and removed a volume, opened it and turned the leaves thoughtfully. Finally he stopped.

'Ah, here it is. Now, let me see . . .' In the photograph before him were assembled the guests, the bride and groom of a wedding – the wedding of Paul Durham, now called Trentam, and Natalya Ivanovna. He paused at his own face in the crowd.

'. . . Fifteen years. Ah well.' And then he found the person he had been looking for: only two to his left and gazing clearly into the camera – the twin sister of the bride, Tatiana Ivanovna; equally lovely and very much in love with the bashful groom, but without the faith that had drawn the other two together.

Isaac sighed. 'Poor girl . . . she was too young to be so sad.' He gazed at the photograph for long minutes before finally closing the book and replacing it on the shelf. 'And now she has found the boy again, and he remembers . . . remembers her or his mother. Maybe he himself does not know which.' He turned to his wife. 'Irène, have you been praying for them?'

'Yes, Isaac,' she replied. 'I have prayed all that you asked me to and more. The Lord is with them as they talk. He will help the boy to understand; it is in his hands.'

Isaac nodded. 'You are right, my dear – as for me, the spirit is willing but the flesh . . . needs a little more sleep these days. But now I shall pray too, and our Father in heaven will hear our prayers and answer us both.'

At that moment the outside door opened and Jonathan entered the room. In response to their questioning looks, he reassured them.

'Paul is safe. We made the rendezvous as arranged and I have taken him to talk with the elders. The disk is being decoded and he will speak to the Church in less than an hour's time. People are already gathering.' He paused for breath and looked around the room. 'Where are the boy and the woman?'

Isaac indicated the door leading into the rest of the house. 'They are together, in the guest room, my son.'

'You left them alone? Together?' Jonathan exclaimed, with an air of despair. 'Father, there's no knowing what he might tell her!' He crossed the room towards the door.

'Jonathan!' Isaac's voice was firm. It halted the younger man in his tracks. 'You must not go in there. It is important for them both to talk together – alone. The boy will not betray us. Neither, I suspect, will the woman.'

'Father, how could you possibly know that?' Jonathan was not convinced.

Isaac leaned back in his chair and sighed. 'My son, do you have no respect for my judgement? Am I so old that you regard me as a fool who no longer sees what is happening around him nor remembers anything that has gone before? I tell you that I know them both. And I know what you do not; she is his mother's twin sister and will not betray him or us. It was the Lord's will that they should meet. And now that they have, who are you to come between them?'

Jonathan gave way before Isaac's rebuke. 'I'm sorry, father, I didn't mean to be disrespectful.' He sat down. 'I have this feeling. I'm not afraid, but . . . I feel that something is about to happen; I don't know what. So far we have managed to keep ahead of the security forces; but they won't give up trying. And this meeting; it's very risky to have all the Church leaders gathered together at a time like this. That woman makes me nervous; she could be the death of us all. . .'

'I know, Jonathan,' his father replied. 'These are testing times; but trust me, and . . . trust the Lord.'

Mark and Tatiana were sitting side by side on the bed. The boy could not take his eyes off the woman as she spoke in a quiet voice, telling him the story of his own childhood; the first five years of his life about which he knew nothing.

She talked softly and with a dullness born of nine years of sadness and regret, hesitant and faltering, searching for the words to explain what she had felt and done all that time ago. Her head was bowed and her eyes fixed on her hands, which she clasped and unclasped in her lap. She was a schoolgirl making her confession, unburdening herself of the guilt weighing heavily upon her. And Mark, as he listened, moved one step further from being a child and one step closer to being a man. His awareness was bringing with it responsibilities he could not help accepting.

'. . . In the fourth year of the war the Knights of the Church were founded to safeguard the Faith, to make sure the truth would not be lost for ever, and the Church went underground. Many whose faith was known were evacuated to the safety of a new planet city, Ekklesia; many more were tortured, imprisoned or died at the hands of the security forces.' She fell silent. For more than a minute the boy waited. Then she continued.

'Your father was one of the twenty Knights of the Inner Circle. For two years he was at the center of the struggle. He saved many lives. Then he met your mother and married. He relinquished his knighthood. A year later your mother, Natasha, had a baby. He was named Mark.'

'As the Empire grew stronger, one by one the last strongholds of the League fell. The struggle had lasted more than twelve years, but now everyone realized that soon opposition would be useless. We pleaded with the few remaining leaders to surrender, to see an end to the violence, but they could not. They had seen their families, their cities, whole nations torn apart for the sake of what they believed in, and for them death was the only way.

'We did what we could. We nursed their sick and hid them from the Empire forces. We helped their families, although many starved. We were so weak, and we knew we could not fight. The Empire knew the Church was helping the League. They were only waiting for an opportunity to crush us completely, although for the time being we were useful to them also. Many of our number served in their hospitals.

'The last year of the war found us in Diakos. You were just five years old. In the city the Church was sheltering some seventy or eighty refugees, the wounded and their families. Your father held a high position and had been under suspicion for some time. One evening, when he had left the house, a security squad came and took us away: you, your mother and myself.'

She looked up and glanced at Mark. Her eyes were filling with tears which she held back. 'They questioned her, but she told them nothing and then . . . and then . . .' She bit her lip, '. . . they took her away . . .' Her words dissolved into a painful, wretched sobbing. Mark moved closer and put his hand on hers. She cried uncontrollably and he felt again a choking tightness in his own throat. After a while she quieted.

'They made me watch from another room. She could not see me, but I saw . . . everything. She never opened her mouth, not even to cry out. When they had finished with her they came and took you away. They made me watch again as they used the drugs, but you knew nothing. They made your mother watch as they increased the dose . . . they would have killed you. I could hear her crying for help, begging them to stop, and I knew . . . I knew what they wanted to know. I told them everything and they stopped. Then they took me away. I went willingly; there was no fight left in me. I never saw you, Natasha or Paul again.

'When they had the names, they moved in and took the leaders of the Church prisoner and killed those we were sheltering. Then they moved their people out of the city and destroyed it. They bombed the area for four hours. More than two thousand people lived there. Only a handful survived. Most died in the first wave of fires. For those who did not – with the dome destroyed there was only a lingering death from cold and the poisonous gases of the air outside.

'If only I'd known.' She paused, then turned to Mark. 'When I heard your mother begging God to stop them, I thought . . . I thought maybe it was his will that I should tell them. There seemed to be no other way. I didn't know what they would do. All I could think of was you and Natasha . . . and . . .' She lowered her gaze, 'I knew that they would come for me next . . .'

Again she was silent for a long time before looking up and continuing. 'Minutes after they drove me away to the spaceport your father and some other members of the Church stormed the detention center. They managed to overpower the guards. He saved you both, and if I had not gone willingly with our enemies I should have been there too . . .'

She sighed and spoke no more. Mark stared un-seeingly ahead. His dreams were real. They had happened. He recognized them in the story she had told. For the moment he could take no more. His mind was too full

69

of these revelations even to think. Images passed before him without his bidding. Now he knew, and from this knowing there was no return.

20

Lensky was seated at his desk, staring vacantly down at the pad before him. He propped the weight of his head against the knuckles of his right hand and with his thumb absent-mindedly stroked the bristles along the line of his jaw. His expression alternated between a vacant, absorbed wondering and strained concentration. In his left hand he held a pencil with which he doodled aimlessly on the paper on the desk top. He had not moved from this position for more than two hours, and it was now well into the night. His eyes wandered over his scrawlings and he realized with a start that some of the things his roaming mind had put down on the paper were not befitting a Commander of the security forces.

He tore the sheet from the pad and fed it to the shredder built into the desk. Then he put down the pencil and, making two fists, leaned his forehead against them and stared down between the vee of his forearms. Finally he appeared to come to a decision. He flicked a switch on a panel by his right hand.

'Yes, Commander?'

'Get me Admiral Straker on Ganymede.'

'Yessir.' He waited, drumming on the desktop with his left hand. 'Your call is ready, sir; line two.'

He operated another switch, and a video swung up

out of the desktop. The picture appeared. Straker was in a bedjacket in dimly-lit living quarters. He was stocky, swarthy and greying.

'Hullo Lensky, I suppose you know it's the middle of the night here?' His eyes were drooping, half-closed, and he hoped whatever the other had to say wouldn't take long so that he could get back to bed.

'My apologies, Ralph,' Lensky shrugged. 'I find myself in a difficult position and need your help. I'm afraid it won't wait till morning.'

The other waved the apology aside. 'OK, what can I do for you?'

There was a pause. 'How much do you know about operation "Landline"?'

'Nothing; you know your boys never tell us anything.'

'Well . . .' Lensky paused. 'You know at least that it has the highest priority?'

'Sure.'

'We have a problem. One of our agents obtained a list of names that would be most useful to us. Unfortunately, he was neutralized before he could transmit the information. However, he did manage to inform us of some of the details of a rescue mission due to be executed to evacuate the persons concerned, who are all resident here on Titan. This same list has been smuggled onto Titan. This much we know.'

Straker interrupted, 'Look, this is all a little over my head this early in the morning. All I want to know is, where do I come into it?'

Lensky paused. 'Where you come into it, Admiral, is right here. The rebels have to get off Titan sooner or later; there are other circumstances that lead us to believe they will try for sooner. I want the Fifth Fleet in position over Titan by tomorrow morning.'

Straker leaned back in his seat and rubbed his jaw. 'You know, Lensky, you sure have a way of asking.' He sighed. 'You know we just got back from the Martian fiasco?' Lensky nodded. 'Isn't there anybody else you can get to do this? What about Larsson? He's been sitting here twiddling his thumbs for weeks . . .'

'I'm asking you, Ralph . . . because I need the best.'

'Wow, with friends like you . . .'

Lensky picked up the pencil and toyed with it. 'I'm asking you as a favor, Ralph.' He paused and looked up. 'But if I have to, one phone call to the Commissioner will make it an order.' He shrugged. 'You know how irritable he can be if his sleep gets disturbed . . .'

Straker yielded. 'OK, OK. You don't need to twist my arm.' He looked at his watch. 'I'll need three hours to assemble the men on recall, and another fifty minutes to get under way. We'll be with you in just over four hours.'

'Good.' Lensky allowed himself a smile. 'If this operation is successful, you'll be generously rewarded.'

'Thanks a lot,' Straker replied with sarcasm. 'Make sure part of it's a guaranteed good night's sleep.' He reached forward. 'I'll be in touch.' The screen went blank. Lensky leaned back. And if we lose them, he thought, the reward's just as certain.

He spoke into the intercom again. 'Fischer, I want to speak to someone in forensic.'

'Yes, sir.' He glanced at his watch: 23:55. The Fleet should arrive around 04:00. If they delayed longer than that, he had them. 'No reply from the lab, sir.'

'Go through the home numbers.' He spoke tersely, impatient to translate his ideas into action.

What had happened to agent Ivanovna? She had acknowledged their last transmission in the hotel, but since then, silence. He must assume that she was unable to make contact; either she had already been discovered or she was being too closely guarded. But that didn't mean she was useless to him. On the contrary, she would prove indispensable in tracking them down if they remained on Titan. As long as she remained with them, they would eventually be found.

'I have Doctor Kempff, sir. Putting him through now; line two.' Again the video link came into action.

Doctor Kempff was at home. In the background Lensky could hear the strains of classical music.

'Doctor Kempff? I do not believe we have met. I am Commander Lensky. I require your assistance most urgently.' He noticed with satisfaction how the scientist had 'come to attention' at the mention of his name. At least he wouldn't need to browbeat this one.

'Yes, Commander, how may I be of service?'

Lensky continued. 'You will have in your files complete forensic data on agent Tatiana Ivanovna – am I correct?'

'Of course, Commander; in accordance with security policy we have full information on everyone in the security forces. You have a particular interest in this young lady?'

'Indeed I do, Doctor,' he replied, ignoring the faint hint of suggestion in the other's voice; files were regularly tapped for 'unofficial' purposes. 'At the moment she is somewhere in the City, but we have reason to believe that she may be in some difficulty. We need to locate her as soon as possible; her life may depend on it.'

'Our resources are at your disposal, Commander,' the other interjected needlessly; Lensky was fully aware of the extent of his authority.

'Quite . . . Tell me, Doctor, what is the size of your metal hound unit?'

'We have three hounds; two are serviceable, the third is stripped down at the moment for routine maintenance.'

'Hmm . . . and how long would it take to program them with agent Ivanovna's profile?'

Kempff shrugged. 'It's a matter of moments once we are in the laboratory.'

'How long to make the third hound operational?'

'That would take a little longer. A full team, working non-stop, might manage it in under three hours.'

'Excellent!' Lensky said with satisfaction. 'Doctor, you will leave immediately for the laboratory. I shall meet you there in twenty minutes. My secretary will contact the other members of your staff and they will begin reassembly of the third hound. Thank you Doctor, you have been most helpful.'

He broke the link and again spoke to his subordinate. 'Fischer, get in touch with all the forensic team; I want them at the lab now. No excuses. I will be out for the next few hours. Put any incoming calls through to my personal transceiver.'

With that, he rose from the desk, took a hand-weapon from a drawer and secreted it in an inner pocket. He checked his hip holster and crossed the office, turned out the light and left the room. As he did so, across the city those he sought were also about to venture onto the streets.

Jonathan turned to face the other members of the group. They were all ready.

'Now remember, we must make no noise. At this time of night sound travels far. We must travel quickly and silently. Keep close to me and avoid open areas. When we have to cross the main thoroughfares be particularly careful; they will be brightly lit. As far as possible, keep to the shadows. If we're spotted by a patrol, run for the nearest cover and leave everything to me. Have you got that?' They nodded as one. 'All right then, here goes.'

He turned out the light, eased open the door and they saw him for an instant silhouetted in the opening against the dim street lighting; then he was gone. Irène, Tatiana and Mark followed, and last of all Isaac, closing the door soundlessly behind him.

They progressed at an irregular pace for some quarter of an hour, now half-running down exposed stretches, now crouching in the darkness in fear of some faint sound that might be a patrol somewhere close at hand.

Mark recognized that they were retracing the route by which they had approached Isaac's home earlier that day. Now that he knew his father was safe he was no longer worried but impatient to see him again. He had to know more, more than Tatiana could tell. He was too preoccupied to feel afraid. He followed Jonathan's direc-

74

tions carefully, moving from shadow to shadow, listening intently and keeping close behind the women ahead of him.

They waited for many minutes at the junction of Emperor Way and the Third Parallel before Jonathan led them across. During that time five private vehicles passed by in the direction of the center of the City, unusual for so late at night. The time was 00:15. Although Kempff and his staff could not know it, they had passed within yards of their quarry on their way to the laboratory.

The fugitives turned in a direction the boy did not know and several blocks further on arrived at the home of one of the leaders of the Church. In response to a spoken code, the door opened and they were admitted, finding themselves in a large room packed with fifty or sixty people.

The meeting had already begun and a voice (Mark could not see the speaker) was coming from the far end of the room.

'. . . for some of us this news means that our lives can never be the same. But first I will play you the message we have received. It will explain the circumstances that have arisen, and why we must take these precautions. The voice you will hear is that of the White Knight. Please listen carefully to what he has to say. Afterwards my friend here will answer all your questions.' There was a silence, people coughed and shuffled, then a new voice filled the room.

'My dear friends on Titan: Grace to you and peace from God our father and the Lord Jesus Christ. I am sending you this message because it is clear now that some of you are in much danger. Not that this is a cause for alarm. The very fact that you are listening to me now means that you are already close to safety, that our plans so far have gone well. I must explain to you how this danger has arisen. The bearer of this message will tell you what you must do.

'A few hours ago we discovered that one of our top security memory banks had been accessed without authorization, and that there had been an attempt to disguise this fact. The files that had been read contained records of all our dealings with the Church on Titan, together with a list of names of every person in authority there, with brief biographical details.

'At an emergency meeting of the Inner Circle of Knights, we decided that all craft should be grounded until the person who had acquired the information was found. We were unanimous in the view that this was an act of treason. It was logical to assume therefore that he would attempt to relay this information to the Empire which, for reasons you do not need to know, would necessitate leaving Ekklesia and transmitting from near subspace.

'At the same meeting a general rescue plan was proposed and agreed upon; namely to evacuate all the people, along with their families, whose names appeared in the list, and bring them to safety on Ekklesia.

'I now have to inform you that, following this emergency meeting, events have occurred which show the situation to be even more serious. I now know that there is a second traitor, one within the Inner Circle. He had relayed all our discussion to his accomplice in possession of the list. Alerted to our discovery, he pre-empted our safety precautions and left Ekklesia in a small ship with little opposition. By the time he was intercepted he had transmitted news of the rescue plan to Empire forces, although he did not have time to send the names of Church officials in his possession.

'We therefore find ourselves trapped. The general outline of our plan is known to the enemy and to go through with it will mean risking everything. We are forced to enlist the help of someone beyond suspicion on Earth. The danger inherent in our plan is that the co-ordinates for the Planet City will have to be stored in a readable form for programming of the rescue ship, which in this case cannot be one of our own. We have never done this before. Ekklesia's location is known only to me, and I personally program this information into inaccessible files of Charger ship navigational computers.

'If the coordinates of Ekklesia are discovered, our position will be hopeless. The identity of the second traitor is still unknown; he is a member of the Inner Circle, holding knowledge that in the Empire's hands would result in the death of maybe thousands, amongst whom members of the Church on Titan would be the first.

'After much prayer, I have decided to go ahead with the evacuation of Titan as planned, trusting the Lord to keep the knowledge of Ekklesia's location from our enemies.

'My brethren, the man who brings you this message is an old and trusted friend who in the past has served the Lord faithfully as the Crimson Knight. All our hopes rest on him.

'Forgive us, please, we who are sworn to serve you all in the defense of the Faith, for bringing this trial upon you by our lack of perception. I cannot find the words to tell you how sorry I am. May the grace of our Lord Jesus Christ, and the love of God, and the fellowship of the Holy Spirit be with you now and always.

"In His Strength We Stand." '

As the motto of the Knights of the Church closed the message, the room fell quite silent. Lives were changing direction. Aims, ambitions, hopes were forfeit. For those named on the list everyday life had come to an end. Ahead lay a perilous bid for freedom, and new lives in exile on Ekklesia, although that exile would be more wonderful than they could possibly imagine.

The only alternative was imprisonment, torture and death at the hands of the security forces in their relentless pursuit of the total destruction of the Church.

As for Mark, three words were ringing in his head, 'the Crimson Knight.' He remembered Tatiana; '. . . your father was one of the twenty Knights of the Inner Circle . . .' The Inner Circle . . . the phrase echoed hollowly. He was beginning to realize how little he knew about his father and his mother.

77

21

Commander Lensky studied the machine Kempff was bending over. The metal hound was the ultimate in robotics technology. Equipped with exquisitely perceptive sensors, it could follow a chemical profile matched to the one stored in its electronic brain weeks after the trail had been laid. It would lead him to agent Ivanovna, he was confident, in a matter of hours.

In every feature, the machine extended and improved upon the living creature whose name it bore. In addition to its sophisticated array of scent detectors, its eyes – telephoto cameras with light intensifiers for night-sight – could detect its prey at greater range than any flesh-and-blood hunter. Its hearing was acute, enabling it to pinpoint a source with deadly accuracy.

Lensky noted with a grim smile how closely its designers had mimicked nature by placing its weaponry around the squat metal muzzle. Twin lasers nestled in hollows on either side of the upper jaw. Below and behind them, the bulging cheeks concealed the electro-hydraulic pistons that could close the jaw with a crushing power greater than any living carnivore.

Kempff straightened and turned. 'Programming is complete, Commander. Where do you wish the hound to be directed to begin its search?'

Lensky crouched down to scrutinize the beast, and put out his hand to touch the cold, grey metal. He ran his fingers along the barrel of the laser, cool and smooth.

'The Hotel Imperial, emergency exit opening onto Sixth Parallel.' He spoke without turning. Behind him, Doctor Kempff smiled as he moved over to a small console.

'It is a remarkable piece of equipment, is it not Commander Lensky?' He leaned over towards a button, 'And no mere pet.'

Lensky withdrew his hand sharply as the hound came to life. Reacting to the touch of his fingers, it turned to face him and he heard its eyes whirr quietly as it focussed. At the same time, the twin muzzles of the lasers pivoted to converge on his face.

'If yours was the profile in the machine, you would be dead now, Commander.' There was a smugness in his voice that Lensky, from his position, did not care for. He had started slightly and Kempff had had a little fun at his expense. He stood up stiffly, unable quite to turn his back on the hound. A moment later it turned its attention to the laboratory door which had opened at the scientist's command. The hound moved silently across the room and out into the night.

The meeting that Paul Trentam had addressed was now over. The others had departed; only those who needed to know the details of the evacuation remained. Paul was studying the map pinned to the wall. A small black ring indicated the pick-up point where the refugees were to assemble shortly before dawn. Isaac was listening attentively as he explained the details of the timing that would have to be tightly adhered to if they were to get off the planet alive.

'I'll have to get into the spaceport and reach the *New England*. Jonathan will come with me; he knows the layout and is my only chance of getting in undetected. He's also prepared a little diversion we can arrange once we're inside.

'Everyone else must be assembled at the rendezvous by five thirty a.m. When we lift off from the spaceport we'll bring out behind us every ship the Empire can muster. There'll be no time to wait for latecomers. We'll approach from the west, flying down this ravine . . . here.' He traced the contours. 'That should shield us from ground-based scanners and mean they'll have to waste precious time with high level passes to pick us up. I think we can count on a minute, maybe a minute and a half, to get everyone on board.'

One of the leaders interrupted. 'What about Sun City?'

'Sun City?' Paul threw him a questioning glance. 'I don't see how that affects us at all.'

'But they continuously monitor this area of Titan. They have a whole array of infra-red sensors checking surface temperature. They'll spot your exhaust heat the moment you leave the spaceport.'

Paul gaped as this awful realization dawned. 'We never . . . we just didn't take it into account.' He thought out loud. 'That means they'll have a constant fix on our position. We'll be sitting ducks.' He lapsed into silence. 'It's too late to change now, and even if it wasn't, I don't see what else we can do. We could never get so many people into the spaceport undetected. It has to be just one or two.' He frowned with concentration, 'There's got to be a way . . .'

He closed his eyes in silent prayer. They had been brought this far. Now they needed help. How could they stop the monitoring? They needed time to pick everyone up. But how, how?

He was interrupted; Jonathan had come over. He looked from one expression to the other.

'What's wrong?'

Paul met his steady gaze, 'We forgot about Sun City; it monitors this whole region. It will tell the pursuit craft exactly where to find us. We won't have time to make the pick-up.'

Jonathan looked at the map and nodded. 'It makes quite a difference. Empire fighters scramble in less than a minute. We'll have only half as long as we counted on.' The three stood there helplessly.

'Paul?'

Paul Trentam's head jerked up, and he saw the woman standing there. 'Natasha! . . .' Even as the name was on his lips he realized he was wrong. 'Tanya!' He stood in stunned silence, the color draining from his face. The pencil he was holding clattered onto the table. Finally, with what seemed an immense effort, he stepped towards her and took her by the shoulders. His words came in gasps. 'Tanya. I thought . . . but everyone was . . .'

She smiled, but it was an admission. 'No, Paul. I was worth more to them alive. I . . . I proved my loyalty.' The two stood regarding one another; his hands slipped from her shoulders. The expression on his face was one of utter disbelief. 'You see . . . once I'd started . . . there was no going back. I couldn't help myself.' She was trembling, shaking almost. 'It's been nine years.'

Her head dropped, she could not bear to meet his gaze. 'I'm sorry Paul, I'm so sorry.' Irène had come across the room and laid her hand gently on the woman's shoulder. Tanya turned towards her to hide her tears.

'I've got it!' Jonathan exclaimed. Paul Trentam turned. He tried to focus, to gather his thoughts. His mind was in turmoil. There were too many things fighting for his attention. He glanced back at Tatiana Ivanovna. Irène was leading her away, speaking gently to her. He had forgotten how closely identical the twins had been. All his memories, the ones he had buried for his own survival, and the boy's, had come to life. He fought them down and focussed on the face in front of him. Jonathan was talking excitedly to him. He could hear sounds, but make no sense.

'What?'

'The radio link between Sun City and the ground. The antenna is here,' he stabbed a finger on the map. 'We'll fly right over it. It's an easy target, more than fifty meters high; there's nothing else like it in the entire City.'

'You mean . . . you think you could hit it with the ship's laser?'

81

'Easy.'

'We'd be accelerating as we passed it; you'd only have one chance.'

'I could do it.'

Paul accepted. 'I don't suppose we really have a choice. Have you ever used a laser before?'

Jonathan beamed. 'I'm a demolition engineer; we use them all the time.'

Paul managed a smile. 'Then you're on.' He paused. 'It doesn't solve the problem entirely, though; it won't take them long to establish a direct link with the pilots. They can still tell them where we are.'

'That's true,' Jonathan agreed, 'A simple voice link from Sun City to the pursuit planes will be easy; but they won't be able to communicate directly with the on-board navigational computers; that has to go via the ground control network. Those coming after us will be forced to rely on their own skills rather than automatic electronic guidance. Those pilots aren't used to relying on their own faculties; everything will take longer. It'll give us a bit more time, maybe enough.'

Paul Trentam nodded. 'It's the best we can do. It'll have to be enough.' He looked at his watch. 'It's almost 01:30. We've covered everything. Now I've got to get some sleep.' He looked around. 'How's Mark?'

'He's fine,' Jonathan reassured him. 'He's been under a lot of stress with all this cloak and dagger business going on around him. And . . . there's that woman. Isaac told me about her. It seems you kept a lot from the boy.'

'All of it; it was for his own good. One word to link us with the affair on Diakos after we'd returned to Earth would have meant death for me . . . and Mark would have been left all alone. We had to leave my wife behind.'

'But I don't understand why he doesn't remember for himself. He must have been five or six then?'

Paul shrugged. 'I don't know either. He was interrogated; they gave him truth drugs. We had to leave Natasha behind, the city was being bombed out of existence; it could be any one of those things that is too

82

frightening to remember. He just went blank, except for his nightmares, and he couldn't make sense of those.'

'Well, he knows now. I don't know how much she told him, but they were alone together talking for more than an hour when I came to meet you. He even looked different afterwards.'

'He'll be all right. When this is all over I'll tell him everything; we could never go back to Earth now. It'll be good to talk. I only ever told one person; just after we were found. We'd crash landed and I was badly wounded. I had to explain; they couldn't risk sheltering an enemy agent. Afterwards I even had to burn Natasha's photograph, the only thing of hers I had left.'

He sighed. 'I don't want to think about it any more just now; there are too many other things to worry about. Let's get back to Isaac's.'

22

Commander Lensky and Doctor Kempff were seated at a control console in the laboratory. A section of the wall panelling facing them had slid back, revealing a large screen. They were both following the moving picture displayed there. The scene was constantly changing, flowing past them as the hound moved along the deserted streets. They were looking through its eyes. The darkest corners appeared clearly lit in the image synthesized by its electronic brain.

At the moment, the only sounds were the barely perceptible workings of the machinery driving the robot forwards. Everything else was silent. The laboratory was in darkness apart from the picture on the wall and a small pool of light in the far corner where the third hound was being assembled, too slowly, it now appeared, to play any part.

'How recent is the trail that the hound is following at this point?' Lensky asked.

'It's impossible to say.' The scientist tapped some keys on the panel in front of him and a family of graphs appeared on a small monitor in the console. 'These lines show the concentrations of individual components in the profile. As you can see, some are higher than others. That merely reflects their initial levels and different durabilities, but the important point to notice is that without exception all the curves mount steadily as a general trend since the hound picked up the trail at the hotel. This graph,' he touched the keyboard again, 'combines all those elements to give us the profile as a whole. It shows even more clearly how the signal is steadily becoming stronger and emerging from the "noise" of all the other scents around. There is no doubt, Commander, that the hound is steadily overhauling its prey. It is only a matter of time.'

'Good.' Lensky rubbed his eyes and then wiped them with a handkerchief. 'When it catches up with them, I don't want you to send it in right away. Agent Ivanovna's profile was the only one available to us, but she herself must not be harmed. I am more interested in the people who will be with her. They are the ones who have the information I want. They must be identified and immobilized until a patrol can be sent to bring them in.'

He yawned and looked at his watch. It read 01:58.

'Doctor Kempff, I am very tired and anticipate a long day ahead of me. Do you have a sick bay attached to the laboratory where I can rest for a while? I can be of no assistance at this stage of the search, but I must be on hand when the hound makes contact.'

'Certainly, Commander. Gregson will show you where the resting room is.' He indicated one of the team assembling the third hound. 'I will call you the moment there are any developments.'

The fugitives had made their way back across the City without incident and reached the safety of home. Paul and Isaac were alone in the living room; the others were already preparing for bed. The curtains were drawn. A reading lamp stood on the table between the two men, shedding a warm and comforting light that reached into the shadows around the room.

Paul closed his eyes and felt the stillness. Despite their situation, it seemed this was a time for peace – or maybe it was because of . . . Eventually Isaac stirred and rose from his seat. He went over to the far side of the room and in the near-darkness Paul saw him take something from inside a drawer. He returned to the table and took his place again. Paul's gaze fell with recognition on the brown cloth bag that he placed by the lamp.

The old man spoke gently. 'It is time to return these to you.'

Paul glanced up and then back to the center of the table. There lay the tools of his trade. They called to him like a long-lost friend. He wanted to reach out and take them, to welcome them back as his own.

But they were also a gauntlet; the challenge of old to stand and do battle. They belonged to the days before Natasha. Although he dwelt for a moment on these ideas, he realized that he had already taken up that gauntlet. The challenge had come to him the day before, on Earth, in a peaceful moment similar to this. Then too it had been brought to him by a trusted friend. He had accepted and put an end to nine years of waiting.

He lifted the bound weapons from where they lay and felt their weight in his hands. His mind went back to the last time he had held them, on the eve of his wedding. Then they had passed in the other direction. He completed the undoing of that earlier day by loosening the cord that bound the cloth. It opened in his hands to reveal . . . what he knew so well. In his left, the shield, in his right, the baraq of a Knight of the Church. His baraq and his shield that would respond to every touch and pressure, every nuance of gesture: the weapons of personal combat.

He had feared they would be returned to him. He had never really left them or the things they stood for. They could have claimed him at any time. Now, in God's time, they had. He could tell whose hand had really brought them to him, or him to them. He knew who had touched him inside with the needs of his friends. And despite his tiredness and his knowledge of what tomorrow would hold, despite the sadness he had struggled with through the years, he now accepted it. He felt satisfied; it was good.

'You remember . . .'

'Yes, Isaac, I remember.'

The old man carried on with enthusiasm. 'We were unbeatable . . .' Then he thought better of it as he caught Paul's mood. He shrugged and finished lamely, 'I'll do all I can to help.'

Paul felt a rush of emotion; he was the same Isaac he'd always known, the very same. When they fought, they fought as one man.

'I know, Isaac,' he replied. 'And I need your help now just as much as I ever did.'

Mark was lying awake in the darkened bedroom. He felt sick and exhausted, but his excitement would not let him sleep. He listened to the soft murmur of conversation filtering through from the living room where his father and Isaac were talking. At last all was quiet. He heard doors open and close quietly and then his father came into the room.

He crossed to the window and stood by the curtains. By the light slanting in through a gap between the two drapes, he was looking at something he held in his hands. Mark caught the reflection of burnished metal. His father weighed the object first in one palm, then the other. He turned it over, gripped it, adjusted his hold, turned and flexed his wrist and then examined it again.

'Dad?'

'Mark. I thought you'd be asleep by now. Did I wake you when I came in?' He came across and sat on the bed.

'No, Dad, I can't get to sleep. I wanted to ask you something.'

'What's bothering you?'

'Well, you know I had a talk with Tatiana Ivanovna?'

Paul Trentam nodded. 'Yes, Jonathan told me after the meeting.'

'One of the things she told me was that you came and got me and Mom when those people had taken us away. She said that you got us both out of there . . .'

'That's right; I had some help from our friends in the Church. When we arrived, we managed to find you and your mother, but Tanya had disappeared.'

'Well, if we all got away . . .' He struggled, afraid almost to ask the question because of the answer it might have. 'What happened to Mom? Why didn't she get back to Earth with us?'

His father was very quiet for a while.

'When we got out of the detention center, we, that is, you, your mother, me and the eight people who had helped us, decided to make for the spaceport. That was the only way out of Diakos, and we knew that if we stayed, sooner or later we'd be recaptured.

'Of the others, five had to go home first to pick up their families. We waited as long as we dared for them to rejoin us but it was not safe to stay in one place for very long. Eventually only three returned, with their wives and children. We started to make our way across the city.

'We still had quite a way to go when the Empire started to bomb. When the first wave came over we were caught on the street. Several of the shells came very close and we were thrown off our feet by the shock wave. I was hit in the shoulder by something thrown up by the blast. We were all dazed.

'When we started to come around, we found that you had wandered off. We'd been thrown in different directions and you'd lost us. The others went on. Your mother and I started to search. You were only two streets away when she found you. By that time the whole city was on fire. The few buildings still standing were gutted. As she got to you, you were kneeling where you'd fallen in the road.

'The building in front of you began to keel over. There was no time to pick you up and carry you clear. She managed to cover you with her own body.' There was a long silence.

'When the dust settled, all I could see was a pile of rubble. When I got closer I could hear you crying, and then I saw your mother's arm sticking up out of the wreckage. I dragged some of the debris aside and managed to pull you both clear.

'It was a miracle that you were both alive. You were hardly grazed but Natasha . . . One of her legs was broken and she hurt when she breathed in. I knew I couldn't carry her. My shoulder was bleeding and beginning to stiffen. She knew it too. She made me promise to get you away. I didn't know what I was saying. Then we saw a patrol at the far end of the street. They were looking for us. In a few moments they would turn in our direction. She hugged you, and while she was holding you she was gazing at me. Her eyes were pleading with me to take you from her, to pick you up and run, to leave her.

'She held you out at arm's length, looking at you, but towards me. At the last she could not let you go, she needed me to take you. I pulled you apart. Then I was running. At the far end of the street I turned; I saw them reach her. Two stayed with her, three came after us. I ran again. I ran until the pain in my shoulder from carrying you was unbearable. Then I rested for a minute before going on. I remember sitting on a pile of rubble and thinking I would never get up.

'When we reached the spaceport, I could see our friends pinned down behind a buggy close to a transporter ship. Some were on board, keeping back the guards by sweeping the tarmac with the craft's laser. The others were running, one by one, the fifty yards to the ship. I saw two who made it, one who didn't.

'For us, it was a diversion. We got into a hangar unnoticed. I loaded you aboard a fighter and sedated you with a pre-jump shot. I blasted a hole in the roof and we took off through it. In the confusion the last of the party on the ground made it to safety. They lifted off close behind us.

'We made the jump to Earth but on the way in we hit something – a satellite, space debris – I don't know. We had to eject. The fighter burned up. I passed out. When I came to, we'd landed. We were found the next morning, and by friends. The rest you know.'

Mark was silent. His eyes were staring into the darkness.

'You left her behind.'

His father sighed. He had voiced the same accusation for the past nine years.

'Yes.'

He felt the boy withdraw from him and into himself, beginning to hold back his love as a punishment. As the silence deepened and the distance between them widened, he searched for more words to say.

'Mark.' He put out his hand and laid it on the boy's arm. 'I don't expect you to understand this now, but please listen. The fighter we flew out in was designed for a three-man crew. When we drifted down to Earth we landed in a small forest. We were in the front two seats. When I came around, I dragged you out of the cockpit. You were behind me. Just behind you, the cabin had been torn open and a section of a thick bough had been driven up through the floor and out through the roof before snapping away. That was where your mother would have been sitting.

'I don't know where she is now, but I believe that was not the time for the Lord to call her to be with him. Whatever has happened to her, I believe that our Father knows. He's allowed it; and because I know he loves her, even more than I do, I know that it must be the best for her.'

Mark's head rolled to face the window and Paul watched as the first tear slid down his cheek and onto the pillow. They were silent tears, and bitter.

His father got up and walked over to his own bed, undressed and got into bed. As he lay in the stillness, he felt the full anguish of love at the suffering of his child – the anguish his heavenly Father had known while his Son hung upon the cross. The same pain of love that had brought Him to that place.

Far out beyond the orbit of the planet Saturn, space stretched endlessly, cold, dark and silent. Into the emptiness the mighty flagship *Conqueror* emerged, its wedge-shaped bulk slicing into the space-time continuum. A faint tremor passed along its craggy form as it broke the light barrier. On the bridge, Admiral Straker gazed ahead into the darkness. In the room around him his senior officers guided the craft forward, making it respond to his every command.

On the fifteen decks below him, an army of crewmen and robots toiled in the service of the death ship, enabling it to move, seek out and destroy those who opposed the rule of the Empire.

In the armory, the depleted plasma banks that had so recently despatched hundreds of young insurgents in the Martian campaign, were now fully recharged. There was no visible sign of the death that had been dealt out except a single figure mounting steadily, counting the number of volleys fired since the last overhaul.

Warfare had become clean, efficient. No blood stained Admiral Straker's hands. Those barbaric elements had been removed. He carried out his judgements from a distance. So it was that he could still sleep quietly at night, feel clean, respectable, and above all, right. No shock of human suffering could ever pierce the web of his illusions. He was powerful, remote. Having eyes, he would never see, and ears, never hear.

Other craft appeared until finally a total of twelve warships powered in towards the speck that was Titan. As Mark and his father slept on, the sledgehammer that was the Fifth Fleet swung closer.

Lensky dragged himself from the depths of sleep and opened his eyes. Kempff was shaking him by the shoulder, 'Commander, you must come now. The hound is very close. Here . . .' He handed him a towel and motioned him towards a sink. 'Use this. I must return to the control console.' Lensky splashed cold water over his face, the shock jarring him awake, and then rubbed his face dry vigorously. When he emerged into the laboratory, Kempff called across to him.

'A few moments ago the hound came across a new, stronger trail; here – at the junction of Emperor Way and the Third Parallel. It is superimposed on the weaker signal that it had been following. A second trace of intermediate strength led off into the residential district to the north. There is only one possible interpretation. The signal we were following initially is the oldest scent. More recently, your agent retraced her steps to this junction and then headed off northwards, returning sometime later along the same path to the place where she had first been taken. That cannot now be far away, the profile is so clear. It is only a matter of minutes.'

Lensky sat down beside the scientist. A few moments

later his wrist transceiver bleeped twice. He pressed a button.

'Fischer here, sir. I've just received a communication from Admiral Straker. The Fleet came out of hyperspace seven minutes ago at 04:11 and is approaching the planet now, sir.'

'Good. My orders are to take up a stationary orbit twenty-five kilometers above Titan's surface, directly over the City. I want to be informed when they are in position; they'll receive further instructions then.'

'Yes, sir.'

Lensky leaned his weight on his elbows and closed his eyes. Tired as he was, he could still feel the satisfaction of knowing that this time there was no escape. The fugitives were still in the City. If they remained there any longer, he would find them, and very soon. If they tried to leave they would find the Fifth Fleet barring their way. Only a fool would not surrender in face of certain death. He would take them alive and then total victory would be his.

24

Jonathan, Isaac, Irène and Mark's father were in the living room. They were sitting around the table, still and quiet; there was nothing left to be said that could be said in the short time remaining to them.

Irène rose. 'It's time to wake the others.'

Paul got up hastily from his seat. 'Please, I would like

to speak to Tanya. There is something I must say to her before we leave, and there may never be another time.'

Irène nodded. 'I will wake Mark. But hurry; we haven't long now.'

He went out into the corridor, knocked on the door, waited, and then opened it. Tatiana was standing by the window, she had drawn back the curtains. She did not turn as he came into the room; her back was to him. For a moment he could not move. The way she stood, resting her weight on one foot, her head tilted to one side – everything about her reminded him so forcefully of Natasha. He closed his eyes and leaned against the door, then after a moment walked over to her.

'Tanya?'

She turned. Her face was expressionless. 'You needn't have come Paul; I never liked goodbyes.' They stared at one another.

He took her hand gently. 'Now that I've found you again after all these years, do you think I'd leave you behind?'

She met his gaze. 'It's what you want, isn't it? I remind you too much; of Natasha, of the past. It's gone, Paul. I'd only make it harder for you by being around. I'm not Natasha, and I never will be. Sometimes I wish I was. She was so strong.' She was staring at the ground and now she pulled her hand away from him. They stood there awkwardly while he tried to think what to say.

'Tanya, I don't blame you for what happened, no one does. You aren't to blame for the evil in others. How can I condemn you for weakness when I am so weak myself? Our strength is only in the Lord. Come with us to Ekklesia and leave all this behind.'

Her eyes turned to meet his, but only for an instant.

'Paul, I want to come with you. I do . . . Oh!' she gasped, her eyes staring. He followed the direction of her gaze to the window.

There, inches away, were the demonic features of the hunter killer that had pursued them across the city, its unblinking eyes watching them intently. They froze, and the hound dropped out of sight.

The truth hit her, 'Paul,' she gripped him painfully, 'don't leave me.' Panic was wild in her eyes. 'Please, they'll kill me . . .'

'I won't.' He held her tightly. 'You're coming with us.' They fled into the living room where the others were waiting.

'Get away from the windows!' Paul waved them back. 'And keep below the level of the sills. Isaac, your shield and baraq. Get them and be ready.'

'What . . .?' Jonathan began to form the question.

'There's a metal hound outside. It's seen us both. They'll already be on their way. We must leave now, but first I'll have to deal with the machine.'

'How did it find us?'

'It's my fault,' Tatiana burst in. 'They have my profile. We came here on foot. I should've realized.'

Paul was talking quickly and quietly to Isaac. 'When I engage the hound, you and the others leave by the back entrance to the garage and get into the car. Give me one minute, no more. If I can't get to you by then, you must leave before the patrol arrives. Then it's up to you to fly the *New England* out.' He handed him a package. 'Here; you take the disked coordinates. They've been decoded. The navigational computer will accept them.' The old man did not protest. Paul turned to Jonathan. 'If you see the hound at all once you're in the car, it means I've lost. You must leave. You should be able to shake it off.'

On the table lay a cloth bag wrapped around and bound by a leather thong, which he proceeded to untie.

'Mark, come here a minute.' His son watched as the cloth unfolded to reveal two identical metal cylinders. His father took one in each hand and spoke to him in a low voice so that the others could not hear.

'Whatever happens, I want you to stay with Tanya. I want you to look after her. You understand.'

'Yes,' Mark whispered. 'I understand.' He wanted to

94

ask, 'Does it have to be you who goes out there?' but he already knew the answer.

Paul nodded as if to say 'then I can do what has to be done.' He turned to them all. 'Now, stand away from the door.' He looked down to the objects in his grasp and then up towards them all. 'Pray for me.' The door opened and he was gone.

Lensky was leaning forward in his chair, his tiredness vanished. 'The patrol will be there in a few minutes. We've got them, Doctor, we've got them.'

Kempff had remained cool. 'Someone just left the house; that was the sound of a door closing. The hound is moving around to the front to investigate.' The corner of the house vanished off the right of the picture. They were looking diagonally across the street, in the middle of which a single figure stood facing them.

'That's him – Trentam!' Lensky exclaimed. The adversaries regarded one another.

'What are your instructions, Commander?'

'He must be prevented from escaping, but I want him alive. Avoid body wounds.'

'Would the right upper arm be satisfactory?' the scientist inquired, as if selecting an item from a menu.

'Yes, Doctor,' Lensky grinned, 'most satisfactory.'

Kempff's hands moved over the computer keyboard. The hound circled around, keeping the same distance, but moving out into the street so that there were no obstacles between it and its prey.

Paul Trentam regarded the robot unflinchingly. The fact that it had not killed him earlier in the house meant, he knew, that they intended to take him alive. He squeezed a section of the metal rod in his left hand, and a ring of crimson light appeared, hanging in space before him, a meter in diameter. It followed his movements as he flexed his wrist, having as its pivot the cylinder held in his grip. From the other side it was invisible, but it marked the rim of the shield behind which his body was protected.

His right arm hung slightly flexed at his side, holding his other weapon, the baraq of a Knight of the Inner Circle.

The hound stepped into the road and faced him squarely. He noticed the lower jaw open a fraction. His body tensed and he flung out a desperate prayer. The hound took one step forward slowly, then, as it moved into perfect equilibrium, bounded forwards. He heard the hiss of pneumatic rams as it leapt, its jaws gaping wide for the flesh of his arm.

As it powered forwards and upwards he dropped to his right knee, swung the shield up and across his body, brought his other fist up into a double-handed grip, and took the impact of the hound inches above his head. There was a heavy clang of reverberating metal and the machine somersaulted higher, carried on by its own momentum and by the additional upward thrust of the blow.

For long seconds, it twisted in the air. Then it crashed to the street, shattering the pavement, and skittered to rest. Paul swung the shield on through after the impact and pivoted his body around behind it to face the hound. Both man and machine regained their feet, but from a twisted linkage in the hindleg on which the robot had fallen, hydraulic fluid dripped onto the street.

The hound surged forwards again, but more slowly this time and with a hint of awkwardness in its gait. As it approached, Paul swung his right hand down to the floor and lifted the shield a fraction. There was a blinding flash, from which the shield protected him, and the robot kept coming, but now guided only by its hearing, its sensitive light detectors fused or momentarily saturated by the sudden intense burst of energy.

At the last instant, Paul Trentam sidestepped and, as the hound drew level, brought the edge of his shield crushing down on the back of its neck. The impulse of the blow momentarily forced it to its knees, and he brought the muzzle of the baraq up against the first vertebra, angled forwards into the skull, and squeezed. A searing violet beam flooded the metal chamber. The hound pitched forwards, its movements jerky and uncoordinated, the memory banks of its silicon brain wiped clean by the ultra-violet radiation. Moments later, in response to a distant hand, it ceased struggling and lay motionless in the street.

Paul Trentam hauled himself to his feet and lurched around the building, his whole frame trembling, gasping for breath. Willing arms maneuvered him into the car and he collapsed, exhausted, as they accelerated away.

Lensky slammed his fist down onto the table.

'Kempff, why the hell can't you give me a straight answer?'

'I don't know, Commander; I mean I don't know what happened,' the scientist spluttered. 'He must have used some sort of photic tube to dazzle the hound, but then I don't know.' He gesticulated at the keyboard, 'Everything's just gone dead. I don't understand it . . . it's impossible.'

'Don't keep saying that!' the other exploded. 'When we can both see perfectly well that it is possible.' He fumed in his chair. 'And what happened when the hound first went in? It just seemed to bounce off him.'

Kempff spread his hands. 'I have no explanation. . . . He must have had some kind of weapon; those cylinders in his hands . . .'

Lensky shoved his chair back and paced the room, his hands clenched so tightly behind his back that the knuckles showed white. This was no longer simply a job to be done, it was now a personal vendetta.

'Dispatch the second hound immediately to pick up the trail before they get too far, and go with someone to bring the other one back so that we can at least see what happened. And next time, Doctor, there must be no mistakes. I want Trentam dead. And Doctor, let me make myself quite clear. From now on, it's either him or you.'

Jonathan twisted together the bare ends of the two cables. The first, red and green striped, wound its way around a bank of relays and disappeared into the junction box. The second, blue, led to the small grey box he had taped to the inside wall of the metal cabinet. It was the last connection. He looked at his watch: 05:07. They were running a little ahead of schedule, having made more of the journey by car than originally planned. The others had been safely dropped close to the rendezvous point. He and Paul had gained entry to the spaceport with no more difficulty than on his last sortie, via a ventilation shaft into the engineering section.

'That's it,' he whispered, and swung the metal door closed, taking care not to break the fine wire leading out to the aerial taped to the underneath of the compartment. Paul Trentam straightened and scanned the pencil beam along the wall. There was no visible sign to show which of the sixteen circuit boxes had been sabotaged.

'Good work, Jonathan. How much time do we have?'

'Plenty,' the other replied. 'Seven or eight minutes to get to the emergency stairwell; we can be in the hangar by 05:15. Then we just bide our time for the best moment, cut the lights, and we're home free.'

Paul smiled wryly. 'I wish I had your confidence.'

Lensky was back in his office. He poured himself a large drink and sat down heavily in his chair. For the first time,

98

he allowed himself to admit that he was frightened. His outburst in the laboratory had been the result of fear. Although he had threatened Kempff with his life, he knew that in reality the death sentence hung uncomfortably over him. With the Commissioner, blame rested solely with the one in charge, and he remembered how he had been introduced to Snider and Johnson. It almost seemed as if fate itself was against him.

He thought back to the days when Grillner had been his superior and he was an eager Lieutenant. No one had asked questions when Grillner disappeared; it was too soon after the Station Q affair to be a coincidence. He had been asked to fill the vacant post and leapt at it. He wondered now which young roughneck was waiting to walk over his grave . . . He poured another drink. This inactivity was unbearable. He must do something.

'Fischer?'

'Yes, sir?'

'Get me Admiral Straker.'

'Yes, sir.'

The swarthy features of the Admiral appeared on the video.

'You again, Lensky? You must be running up a hel-luva phone bill . . .'

Lensky stared at him icily. 'I'm in no mood for joking, Straker.'

'Things not going too well, huh?' He eyed the bottle on the desktop. 'Hey, go easy with that stuff. Relax, everything's under control. There's no way they can get off the planet; not alive, anyway.'

'I know, Ralph, I'm relying on you.' He paused and pushed his finger along the polished wooden surface. 'It's just that — I can't afford to lose this one. You know how it is.'

Straker studied the other's face thoughtfully. 'The screws are really on, hmm?' He leaned forward. 'Listen, Lensky, can anyone else monitor this conversation?'

The other was taken by surprise. 'No, why do you ask?'

Straker continued. 'Well, in that case, take my advice. If anything goes wrong, just "if" mind you, make sure you've at least one bird in hand . . .'

Lensky frowned. 'One bird? You mean a fighter?'

The other nodded. 'There are still one or two places in this solar system where you might drop out of sight.'

'Yes, Ralph; I'll remember that. Thank you. You are quite clear as to my instructions concerning Trentam, if he does get into the air?'

'Sure; offer him one chance; if he refuses to surrender, blast him.'

'Good.' Lensky smiled nervously. 'As I said, I'm relying on you.'

Straker leaned back. 'I know. I'll be in touch.' The screen went blank.

Lensky reached for his drink, half raised it to his lips, and then changed his mind and put it back on the desk. The more he thought about it, the more he liked Straker's idea. He almost smiled again. Straker had never been very bright; if he got away, that would leave only the Admiral to take the blame. He'd be signing his own death warrant to let him off the hook. He looked at his watch: 05:17. This had been the longest night of his life.

Jonathan and Paul were crouched in the darkness near the emergency exit, looking across to where the *New England* stood gleaming in the floodlights. Both were dressed in black and barefoot. In the arena there were a total of nine guards, two groups of three lounging near the canteen, three more walking slowly around. Occasionally a torch shone into a dark corner. They were bored, tired, waiting for the dawn and end of the shift.

Jonathan again checked his watch: 05:19 and 35 seconds.

'We've got to make a move soon.' They had been waiting silently for almost five minutes. Now the deadline was uncomfortably close. Across the other side of the hangar, a door opened and a uniformed figure emerged. In an instant, the attitudes of the guards altered. The three on patrol became alert, conscientious. The other groups dissolved into pairs who moved less-obviously close to the canteen.

Paul shot a glance across to the spaceship. The exit platform was still at ground level. They could swing up into the doorway without operating any machinery. Once inside, they would be out of sight. The new arrival beckoned to the guards, who walked over to him. Jonathan nudged him.

'This could be it. Remember: ten seconds.' He reached inside his back pocket and withdrew a small black box. With thumb and forefinger he pulled out a short aerial. His finger hovered over a single white button.

Lensky addressed the assembled group.

'We are expecting the fugitives to try to leave Titan, which, needless to say, will bring them here. We must be vigilant; it is vital that they be apprehended. Each of you is to stand guard adjacent to one of the seven cargo ships. The other two go around the perimeter and lock the emergency exits. I want this hangar sealed off. I shall be . . . what?' He stopped short as the lights failed. Across the hangar, Paul and Jonathan began the sixty yard sprint.

Lensky shouted, 'Lights! Someone get the emergency lights on. Everyone down, spread out, this might be an attack.'

'Three, four, five . . .' Paul Trentam could not stop the words forming in his mind. The outline of the *New England*, jerking wildly as he ran, loomed larger and closer. Jonathan, younger and fitter, was already five yards ahead.

'Six, seven . . .' They weren't going to make it; when the lights came up they would just have reached the ship. He pushed harder.

'Eight.' Jonathan was there, hauling himself up. He strained to a standstill beneath the opening, his hands felt the lip of the door.

'Nine.' His muscles bulged, pulling him up. His body fell forwards and in.

'Ten . . .' Paul gasped out the word, exhaling the breath he had taken by the emergency exit a lifetime away. The lights came on. He lay on the floor, out of sight below the sill, the blood pounding at his temples and in his ears, and fought back the nausea in his stomach.

Lensky was speaking into his personal transceiver quickly and agitatedly, 'I want a team of engineers checking those circuits; report back as soon as they know what happened.'

One of the guards, getting up from where he had lain on the ground, offered, 'Probably just a power surge, Commander – blew some fuses. Always takes a little while for the back-up system to cut in.'

'Maybe,' Lensky agreed. 'But maybe not. Seal off those exits, now.' His communicator bleeped. 'Lensky,' he snapped. It was Kempff.

'Commander, I have just carried out a preliminary examination of the hound. The matrix tester shows all zeroes on at least four chips. He must have used an ultra-violet flash; all the memory and half the sensorimotor centers have been wiped clean.'

Lensky cut into the explanation. 'Are you trying to tell me the hounds can't stop him, Kempff?'

'No, not at all,' the scientist ventured hastily. 'The next time I shall try to avoid close combat. At a distance the hound is practically invulnerable, and the lasers should prove adequate.'

'I hope so,' Lensky replied grimly. 'I am supervising the security of the spaceport. Report back as soon as the second hound makes contact.'

He closed communication and went back to scouring the hangar. He was looking for something, anything. Against all reason, he was beginning to feel that it was already too late, that Trentam was too far ahead of him.

26

Jonathan crawled across the flight-deck to where Paul Trentam was crouched in a corner, studying the control console at eye-level.

'Everything OK?'

He turned. 'Yes, I think so. It's got the same basic layout as all the other Corporation ships I've flown. It won't be easy without the flight engineer, but I daren't risk powering him up. If they deprogrammed him he wouldn't recognize my voice; he'd take us for intruders and raise the alarm. How about you?'

'The laser's conventional, the controls are self-explanatory. Without actually having had a chance to practice, I'd say I can handle it.'

The other nodded. 'Let me see, 05:27. I'm going to activate the navigational computer and feed in the co-ordinates . . .' He stopped, dismayed. 'Oh no! The disk – I gave it to Isaac.'

'What?'

'In the house, when I went out to deal with the hound. He's got it with him at the rendezvous.'

Jonathan stared at him. 'What are we going to do?'

'There's nothing we can do,' he replied. 'We can't program the jump until we've got that disk. We'll just have to do it as soon as we've made the pick-up.' He clenched his fist. 'It's all extra time, at least another 45 seconds to compute. In this ship, and single-handed, I don't know whether I can keep them off for that long.'

Isaac stared out across the wasteland surrounding the City. They were huddled together under an overhanging cliff in a disused quarry. The nickel ore had long been exhausted and it was slowly filling with the debris of the City's garbage. The last members of their party had just arrived; the church leaders, with their families, numbered fifty-seven in all. He looked from one face to another: strained, anxious, all tired, the younger ones clinging to their parents for security. In its mother's arms, a baby was sleeping. He turned back to the panorama before them. To the left, the narrow rille down which Paul would make his approach. The open mouth of the quarry faced north. To the right, the cliffs that had been cut into the bedrock rose steeply.

Mark was shivering. He was exhausted and had a terrible headache. He had hardly slept at all in the previous hours, but had lain awake turning over in his mind all the things Tatiana and his father had told him. He couldn't get rid of the thought that his mother might be alive.

He looked across to where Tatiana was standing. That was how his mother must look. She was very beautiful. A new commitment was forming in his heart. He was going to look for his mother. If she was still alive, he was going to find her. Now that he knew, he could help his father. They would work together. Nothing was as important as this.

Only now, as he stood waiting for his father to arrive, did he remember to thank God for answering his prayer. For the first time in his life, things were becoming clear. He shivered again and looked across to where the rescue ship would appear. Nothing.

Isaac's eyes narrowed; what was that? He was acutely aware that because of a lapse of memory, the disk, which should have been safely on board the rescue ship, was at the moment nestled in his inner pocket. His imagination might be playing tricks on him. No! There it was again; something was moving along the top of the cliffs. He drew the two squat cylinders from the belt around his waist and scrutinized the skyline.

He measured again the distance from their hiding-place to where the *New England* would touch down. It was an open stretch some hundred meters across and they would be exposed every step of the way. He began to pray quietly, muttering under his breath. He must not alarm the others. The sound of a small rock tumbling down the cliffside, taking with it a cascade of dust and pebbles, came clearly to his ears.

The second metal hound stood at the edge of the plateau. Before it the ground fell away, devoured by the mechanical diggers of the Corporation. Its eyes scanned the heaps of rubbish that were haphazardly filling in the open wound. The scent was strong. Here it would run its prey to earth. As it turned away from the edge, a stone dislodged and skittered down into the quarry. It padded silently along, swinging around the lip of the crater until it reached a steep, winding path that led down into its interior. This was where the trail turned. It began to pick its way down the hillside.

27

Paul Trentam was crouching beside the pilot's seat. Around the flight deck, the control panels, dotted with lights, read him the message that all systems were primed. It only remained to close the airlock door and power-up the main engines. For the third time that minute, he looked at his watch: 05:30 and 55 seconds. Jonathan came over from the other end of the cabin where he could see the back of the guard standing just outside their craft.

'He's not moving, Paul, just standing there. What are we going to do?'

Paul shook his head. 'We can't lift off with him so close. He'd never get clear. We've got to get him away from the ship.' The two regarded one another helplessly. 'There's nothing we can do except pray; it's up to the Lord, now.'

Private Grunfeld was tired. The third watch had dragged interminably, not least because Lensky had been breathing down everyone's necks and consequently they'd had to play it by the book. Now he desperately wanted a cigarette. If he eased back into the shadow under the airlock, no one would see a thing. He felt in his pocket and, without removing the packet, withdrew a cigarette. Matches. He tried the other side. Damn! He'd left them in the canteen. He cursed under his breath and looked around for a source.

Walsh was by the nearest plane, off to his right; he'd have one. He caught his eye and mimed the word, lifting the cigarette clear of his pocket for a moment so the other could see. Walsh reached inside his jacket and took out a small box. Grunfeld gestured him to throw it across, the other indicated a refusal. Where he was standing, he was in plain view of the officers' mess where Lensky was sitting drinking coffee.

Grunfeld sighed. If he wanted them, he was going to have to go across and get them. He looked around the hangar. Lensky was in fact sitting with his back to the window overlooking the area; unless something made him turn round, he'd never see a thing. He fingered the cigarette in his pocket. The others wouldn't give him away; Lensky got on their nerves just as much as he did on his.

He stepped out and around the airlock platform and walked to the tail end of the spaceship, peering into the gloom beneath it as if checking for concealed persons, then he shot a quick glance over in Lensky's direction and padded as quickly and quietly as he could across to the next plane.

He had covered about half the distance when there was a hum of machinery. He half-turned and caught sight of the airlock platform swinging up and closed. The ascending whine of electronic starter motors sang out across the hangar, and then he staggered backwards as the dull boom of power thrusters hit his ears and he felt the blast of scorching air on his face.

The *New England* hung, motionless, above the launch area, the landing skids swung up and into the fuselage; then the power of its engines increased to maximum, the vibrations reverberating around the hangar. It rose on four pillars of fire above the level of the soldiers who stood gaping in amazement, then on to the upper levels and clear of the roof.

Paul Trentam glanced back over his shoulder to where Jonathan was strapping in to the laser command couch, his fingers poised like a concert pianist over the keys of the computer console.

'Ready?'

Jonathan activated the electronic gunsight, gripped the twin directional controls, and nodded. Paul turned, panned the craft around, then hit a sequence of buttons with his right hand. His left held the steering column.

The *New England* surged forwards. The horizon tilted over at a steep angle and the rooftops leapt towards and beneath them, a blur of shapes exploding at them as they skimmed over the city skyline. For an instant, the communications aerial swung into view off to the right. The laser hydraulics brought the barrel around, Jonathan swung the sights down and around to converge on the approaching target, and depressed the firing button. The hiss of coolant sounded in the cabin and a golden thread stretched for an instant between craft and tower. There was a flash of vaporizing steel and as the spaceship hurled by, the mast slowly broke its back one third of the way down its height, keeled over and plummeted to the roof of the building below.

'It's gone!' Jonathan yelled over the roar of the engines, punching his fist into the air. 'We did it Paul, we did it!'

Lensky climbed up and into the cockpit, squeezing down into its narrow confines. With his right hand he adjusted his chin strap and microphone, with his left began to go through the pre-flight procedure, bringing the plane to readiness for take-off. His activities were mirrored in each of the other five pursuit planes: pilots strapped into padded seats; cockpit covers swung down, sealing hermetically. There was the ascending scale of starter motors and then the shrill scream of jet engines. He felt again the disturbing mixture of fear and thrill that he had always known before takeoff. His mouth was dry, the backs of his hands cold and clammy. In the headset built into his helmet, the voice of ComCon droned incessantly.

'OK, pack leader, we are patching you in now to Sun City on direct audio channel. Computer link not available. You're on your own. Do you copy?'

'Roger ComCon.' Lensky flicked a series of switches, then eased the throttles forwards. The plane taxied to the center of the hangar. 'Do you have a fix on their flight path?'

'Yes, we do. Latest information is vector 0.12 kilometers per second, alpha 85 degrees, maintaining zero altitude.'

Lensky turned to look to either side. All six aircraft were in position and waiting. 'Pack leader to pack. Maintain loose formation till visual sighting, then engage as I direct. Aim to disable hyperdrive unit, not total destruct. We want them alive. Do you copy?'

'Roger, pack leader.'

'Will do.'

He pulled back twin levers to his right. The scream of the engines strained higher, powerful rocket boosters cut in, and the planes lifted, as one, up, clear and away from the spaceport.

The *New England* had already left the city behind. Beneath them, the rubble-strewn expansion zone sped by. Paul Trentam was arcing the craft around in a gentle curve. A cleft in the plateau drifted in from the right. The ship banked steeply, Jonathan gulped as the ground fell away, and then the nose dipped down and they hurtled along the ravine, like a bobsled in a run. The horizon canted giddily up towards the vertical. A rock wall loomed and swung away as the craft rolled and plunged along the narrow cleft.

The restraining webbing buffeted the breath from Jonathan's lungs. His fingers dug into the leather arm rests. The gully widened. He was pressed forward against the straps and the flow of movement eased as the *New England* emerged into the basin of the quarry.

With the forward motion killed, the visual world appeared to rebound, receding into the distance. Jonathan closed his eyes and a crystal-clear image of a looming cliff, each pebble, each bush, captured in vivid detail for an instant, sprang to his mind. He opened them again, preferring the illusion to the memory. He looked across to Paul, who appeared to be not nearly so affected. It was always easier for the one in the driver's seat.

Behind them, the airlock had opened and the platform was sinking to ground level. Jonathan hit the release buckle on his seatbelt and lifted himself unsteadily from the chair. Paul was studying the scanner on the VDU. He moved back down the cabin to look out through the doorway.

Towards him across the open ground were running a motley crowd of refugees: men, women and children. At the back, Isaac was encouraging the oldest members. He looked around the rubbish tip. Its lack of dignity seemed somehow appropriate. He was about to turn back into the ship when a movement caught his eye. There, negotiating the lower reaches of the slope into the quarry, was another of the metal hounds. He was stunned for a moment.

'Father!'

Isaac was studying the skyline of the clifftops. He turned at the sound of his son's voice.

Jonathan gesticulated wildly. 'Behind you! Behind!' The old man turned and saw the hound as it reached level ground. He pushed the one he was supporting on in the direction of the ship and turned his back. Jonathan saw a vermilion ring appear before his body. He turned back inside.

'Paul! There's a hound! We've got to help my father.'

The other turned. 'I can't leave the ship. We'd be defenseless. Can you use the shield and baraq?'

Jonathan nodded. 'A little; Isaac showed me.'

'Here.' The cylinders were thrown across to him. 'But, in God's name, be careful; you could just as easily kill Isaac.'

He was gone, stumbling barefoot across the ground, oblivious to the cuts on his feet. As he ran, he squeezed the rod in his left hand, and the crimson ring behind which his friend had sheltered earlier in combat again appeared. Behind him, the first fugitives had just reached the safety of the rescue ship; ahead Isaac stood alone and, beyond him, the hound.

He drew level with his father.

'Jonathan! Thank God.' The two of them backed away slowly from their metal adversary. The hound advanced cautiously, regarding in turn one then the other. An unseen hand directed it to attack, and it bounded towards the old man. Bright blue pencil beams bounced off the convex surface of Isaac's shield and into the piled-up garbage. There was a sizzling sound as they cut through the damp refuse. A fire sprang up. The old man turned the shield with small, sweeping movements, seeking the correct angle. As he did so, the reflected rays arced back and forth, cutting great swathes from the heaped-up rubbish. As the hound leapt at his throat, one of the beams sliced diagonally across its face, passing through

110

the lens and into the right eye. There was a shattering of glass and splutter of short-circuiting electrics. Isaac fell backwards under the machine's weight. The cylinder spun out of his hand and the shield vanished.

The hound, deflected sideways, fell awkwardly to the ground but was up in an instant. Jonathan sprang forward and the death ray that was meant for his father bounced harmlessly away and into the sky.

The hound paused, curbed by its far-off master. Kempff could not risk losing the other eye. Already, with only monocular vision and unable to calculate depth, the robot's effectiveness was severely impaired. Isaac gained a kneeling position. His shield lay eight or nine feet away to the right. The two began to edge around towards it, but Kempff was alert to their intention. The hound moved over to place itself between them and the cylinder.

'The baraq, Jonathan; remember the baraq.'

The metal jaw sagged open, the robot hurled itself against Jonathan's shield, which he was holding out to the side to protect his father. For long seconds, it heaved forwards until finally, sickeningly, Jonathan began to feel his wrist bending backwards. Slowly, the shield tilted back. Soon Isaac would be pinned beneath it. He dropped the weapon, the hound lunged forwards and he thrust his forearm into the gaping jaws inches from his father's throat. Metal teeth sank deep through sinew and muscle, there was a dull crack and Jonathan fell forwards over the metal body. His distant executioner gave the signal, the metal head swung round, and a single blue beam pierced his torso, slicing neatly through flesh and blood. Isaac pressed his baraq to the killer's neck, there was a deadly flash of violet and, too late, the machine fell motionless beneath his son's body.

'Help me! Someone!' The old man stretched out his arm towards the ship, his legs pinned beneath the combined weight of the hound and the limp form of its victim. He trembled as he turned over the palm and inspected the back of his hand, both smeared with blood.

111

'Jonathan, my boy, my son. Live! O God, let him live . . .'

Mark and Tanya had been close to Isaac when he turned to face the hound. They had continued in the direction of the ship and Jonathan had brushed past them as he ran to his father's aid. As they pressed on towards safety Mark had looked back over his shoulder and seen the flash of the robot's lasers during the brief struggle.

The last few people ahead of them were being lifted up into the rescue ship. They were almost at the airlock door when Isaac's plaintive cry came to their ears. Mark looked back in the direction of the call. There seemed to be a jumble of forms, he couldn't quite make it out.

'Come on, move!' The call came from the ship. He froze. Ahead were his father and safety, behind were Jonathan, Isaac and danger. Tanya's expression reflected his own torn desires. She returned his gaze for a long moment and then she was running, back towards where the others lay.

She had been afraid – he had seen that in her eyes – but she had gone back. His father's words cut into his thoughts, 'whatever happens, I want you to stay with Tanya . . . to look after her.' He found himself running.

When he reached the spot where their friends lay, Tanya had already rolled Jonathan to one side and was struggling with the hound. He grabbed hold of the metal carcass and heaved and their combined strength was enough to drag it clear of Isaac's legs. The old man gained his feet shakily. He stooped to gather up the weapons from where they had fallen.

'Jonathan,' he gasped. 'We've got to get him to the ship.' They grappled with the deadweight of the body, Mark at the feet, Isaac and Tanya with an arm each, and began to half-drag, half-carry the lifeless form to safety.

After what seemed an age, Mark felt the weight taken by other hands and was himself lifted and carried the last yards to the ship. Then he was slumped on the floor inside, leaning against Tanya's body with Jonathan lying nearby and the airlock door closing.

Lensky dipped the wing of his fighter to study the terrain speeding beneath. Sun City had given them the coordinates of the place where the fugitives had seemingly gone to ground. They were rapidly approaching that area now. Suddenly the land fell away below them and they were flying over the old nickel workings to the east of the City; a desolate area where refuse was dumped into the hole gouged out of the planet's surface. There, in a clearing amidst the piled-up filth, was the stolen spacecraft.

'Target zero. Target zero. Break formation. Red one, two and three engage at low altitude. Four and five cover the ceiling.' The six aircraft screamed out over the quarry and became mere specks in the distance. Three peeled off and swung around in a wide arc, while the others climbed high into the upper reaches of the atmosphere.

The airlock sealed and Paul Trentam's voice came into the living quarters where the sixty people were huddled.

'This is going to be a rough ride. Make sure the children are strapped in. Everyone else hang on to the fixtures, anything; it's all bolted down.'

As he spoke, the low rumble of the idling motors rose to a muted roar, the ship vibrated with the unleashed energy and edged up into the air. A fighter streaked by overhead and involuntarily Paul ducked. There was no time to gain height; he forced the throttles open and pulled hard on the control column. The *New England* powered forwards, climbing steadily. A pile of debris towered stubbornly ahead and he flinched as the nose burst through the garbage tip, spraying a mulchy slime over the flight-deck windscreen.

Isaac climbed his way up the pitching cabin to the navigator's seat beside him and heaved himself into the chair, buckling in. Paul glanced sideways as the windscreen cleared, and noticed the old man's hand and arm.

'Blood?'

The other nodded, 'Jonathan. He's still alive, but very weak.' Their eyes met for a long moment, then Paul turned back to the view ahead. Isaac reached into an inside pocket and withdrew the package containing the disk, removed and inserted it into the disk drive of the navigational computer.

Paul spoke without turning. 'The pursuit craft have picked us up. There are two groups of three, one low, one high. The defense systems panel is to your right. Use shields in selected areas as necessary, full strength.'

Isaac studied the console. 'I hope you fly as well as you used to. I'm a little slower these days.'

Paul almost smiled. 'We'll manage, Isaac; we always did.'

The *New England* climbed steadily through the atmosphere, Isaac's management of the defense systems equal to the efforts of their pursuers to prevent their escape. Paul Trentam kept the craft soaring upwards, deflecting from this path only to avoid midair collisions with their hunters.

Isaac spoke without turning from the monitor before him. 'Paul, I must rest. I am becoming confused. There are too many of them.' On the screen he was studying, six points of light traced intricate patterns, converging on the target in the center, winging past and arcing away. The three-dimensional image was alive with activity, and he needed all his skill and intuition to direct the mirror shields to the appropriate pre-emptive positions. Now his concentration was beginning to fail.

Paul flicked a glance in the direction of the navigational computer. The green light that would signify readiness to jump was absent.

'Just a few moments more, Isaac. The coordinates aren't in yet.' A bright green beam punched through the starboard wingtip.

'Isaac!'

He pulled the control column up and to the left, the ship keeled over and the star patterns swung dizzily across the windscreen. He caught a glimpse of a light-speckled platform and clutched at an idea. The *New England* thundered towards the engineering complex that was Sun City.

Paul Trentam curbed the thrust of the rocket motors and swung the spaceship down among the bewildering array of towers, booms and platforms. Isaac allowed his hands to fall away from the computer console and leaned back in his chair. He wiped his bloodied hand across his face.

'Praise the Lord.' He was trembling from the shock of his duel with the hound and now the mental acrobatics of space dogfighting. 'Paul, I'm finished,' he gasped, his mouth hanging open slackly, perspiration and blood smeared across his forehead.

'You've done enough, Isaac; I knew you would.' They enjoyed the brief respite afforded them by the protection of the structure through which they were flying; their pursuers would not risk laser warfare amongst the reactor chambers of the platform, without which life on Titan would soon fade.

Paul was piloting the ship and trying to study the navigation console at the same time. Surely they had been in the air longer than forty-five seconds, yet the green light remained obstinately dark. Finally a yellow button in the far corner of the keyboard caught his attention. It was glowing persistently, and for the first time he studied it long enough to read the message on its illuminated surface.

'Disk not ready.'

He leaned over and removed the disk from its drive.

His jaw sagged, he looked over towards the old man, who was leaning back, eyes closed, in his chair, and then quickly turned the disk over and re-inserted it the right way up. They would have to avoid capture for almost another minute.

'Admiral Straker to Paul Trentam on board *New England*.' He jumped in his seat as the intercom came to life. 'Trentam, I know you can hear me. Listen well. On your vertical scanner you will see twelve echoes. This is the Fifth Fleet, of which I am in command. I order you to come alongside and dock with the *Conqueror*. If you refuse, you will be destroyed.' There was a pause. 'You have fifteen seconds to reply, Trentam, beginning now.'

Paul studied the image on the scanner VDU. It was no bluff; a cluster of bright point echoes showed clearly ahead and five kilometers above. His decision was immediate. He leaned over and opened a communications channel.

'Hold your fire, Straker; we're coming out.'

Isaac looked across. 'Paul, we can't give up now.' There was no reply. The *New England* edged forwards between two columns on the rig, ahead was clear space. They slipped out over the side of the raft.

Suddenly Isaac's stomach heaved upwards as the spaceship plummeted like a lead weight in a flat spin. When the stars came back to a semblance of rest, they were beneath the platform and passing along its underside. It stood between them and the fleet above.

Paul Trentam stared up through the overhead observation port. They were gliding beneath a honeycomb array of hexagonal cells, some thirty meters in diameter and almost as deep. At the bottom, they were open to space; at the top, apparently sealed off and in semi-darkness.

'Isaac, what are those?'

The old man was gazing up fixedly. 'We are beneath the photic chambers where the energy from the fusion reactors is converted to white light to illuminate the city below.'

'Then why are they all dark?'

116

'They aren't.' He pointed ahead and Paul could barely see a faint white beam emerging perpendicular to the under-surface. He scanned on either side and distinguished several others dotted around the underneath of the platform.

'But I can hardly see them.'

Isaac nodded. 'The atmosphere is very thin at this height, there is very little to scatter the beam and so make it visible from any other angle.'

Paul slowed their forwards motion uneasily. 'I could fly right through one without even realizing it.'

Isaac nodded. 'You didn't ask my opinion before we came down here.'

Paul turned to his friend, '. . . And if I do?'

The old man raised his eyebrows. 'Then it's all over with us . . . So close to its source, the beam is unendurably bright. We would melt in an instant.'

Paul turned back to his scanner. 'We've got company.'

Falling past the levels of Sun City and pivoting about its vertical axis, was Lensky's fighter, with two others just above it. Paul eased the control column back a little and touched the vertical thrust button for an instant, and the *New England* slid back and up into the cell above it.

29

The fugitive spaceship hung in semi-darkness in its hexagonal chamber. In the dimly-illuminated flight deck Paul and Isaac prayed fervently and watched for the green indicator. Only meters away, a raging inferno hung over their heads. The time was precisely 05:39. On the planet below, the new day began to dawn. The subdued lighting of the night, which had kept the city comfortably warm, began to gain strength and brighten to its daytime level. One by one, heavy shields pivoted about their diagonals and the hexagonal cells of Sun City flooded with an intense white light.

The three searcher planes edged forwards beneath the giant honeycomb, inspecting each opening in turn for the quarry they sought. With the superiority of numbers brought to nothing, Lensky began to feel uneasy. They were on equal terms now: death could come to each, or all, in an instant. Every few seconds, a new shaft of light flooded down from the array of over a hundred chambers. The sequence seemed unpredictable; there was no warning. He began to sweat as he edged his craft around one of the faintly shimmering pillars. Odd that something so bright should appear so dim.

Ahead and to his left, Red 4 nudged into position beneath a new tube. The pilot glanced up and into the empty cell and, too late, noticed a hairline crack appear at its perimeter. Lensky flung his arm up to protect his eyes as the blinding flash of the plane's immolation seared through the visor of his helmet. Supercooled fragments of molten metal, frozen the instant they left the beam, ricocheted off the fuselage of his ship. He blinked and shook his head. He was quite blind, twin blue pools hovered before his eyes.

To his right, Red 5's gaze had been averted at the critical moment. Thus it was that he clearly saw the *New England* emerge from its hiding place only two cells ahead of where Lensky's craft hung motionless, paralyzed. He saw the flare of its rocket motors and identified the bulge of the hyperdrive housing. As the other ship surged forwards, he accelerated after it, swinging across towards the left, in and behind his target. As his plane flew into a pale white shaft, his finger closed on the firing button.

The *New England* emerged from beneath Sun City

like a bullet from a gun, streaking towards light speed. Five kilometres overhead, the deadly arsenal of the flagship *Conqueror* came to bear. Paul Trentam stared fixedly ahead, watching the digital vector readout, his finger poised over the light-drive button. Isaac yelled across.

'Paul! We've got a warning light on the hyperdrive.'

The first fusillade of pulsed lasers struck the craft amidships, the mirror shields buckled and fell.

'We've got to go!'

He punched the button – a mighty hand seized the ship, and tore it free of space and time.

Straker watched as the spot of light vanished from their screens.

'Oh no! We lost 'em, and from right under our noses.' He wiped the back of his hands. 'We'll never be able to fake this one. Sun City must've seen the lot.' He paced the bridge, silent, frowning.

'Aircraft on scanner, sir.' His junior officer drew his attention. 'Coming out from under the complex now, sir.'

'Open communications', he snapped. 'Straker here, identify yourself.'

A voice came back weak, tired and pleasantly familiar.

'Lensky here, Straker. I take it they got away?'

The Admiral smiled broadly. Maybe things didn't look so bad after all. 'They sure did. Where were you when all the shooting was going on Lensky?'

'I was blinded by the flash as Red 4 burned up. It

still hasn't cleared properly, but I couldn't risk staying under that thing any longer.'

Straker was positively grinning. 'Well, I'm glad to see you took my advice anyway. Things wouldn't look too good for you around here just now.'

'You're right, Ralph – and thank you. I couldn't get away without your help.'

'Think nothing of it.' Straker turned to his weapons officer, 'Blast him.'

'Commander Lensky, sir?'

'You heard me.'

'What was that, Ralph?' the other's voice came for the last time.

Straker smiled, 'Just saying goodbye, Lensky, just saying goodbye.'

31

The last of the refugees had safely left the ship, and Tanya and Paul were left alone in the spaceport reception area. They were seated at a small table drinking coffee. Paul admired the dark beauty of her face once more, so like Natasha's, and imagined the warmth of the woman he had not held for more than nine years.

'I'm going back, Paul.'

He was startled from his reverie. 'What?'

She smiled, 'I'm going back.'

'But why?' He gaped and shrugged his shoulders. 'You've waited nine years for this. It's yours; you deserve it.'

She toyed with the spoon in her saucer. 'There's something I haven't told you.'

'There can't be anything that important.'

She met and held his gaze. 'Just one.' Her eyes were dark and serious and he saw again the shadow of sadness that had so recently lifted from her features.

'Natasha?'

She nodded. 'She's alive, Paul.' He stared unbelievingly. 'She's alive. If I go back, I can find out where.'

'How?'

'I'm not sure exactly; I'll find a way.'

His mind was several thoughts behind her. He tried again to string the words together into sense. 'No . . . how do you know?'

'I saw her name. She passed through Titan being transported to Earth seven weeks ago.'

'Earth?' he exclaimed, 'If I'd known . . .'

'If you'd known,' she interrupted, 'you'd still be there now looking for her.'

He was dazed, but one certainty stared him in the face. 'I can't ever go back there, Tanya, after this.'

'I know,' she smiled. 'That's why it has to be me. I'm the only one who can go back and not face certain death. I'll take this technician traitor who caused all this trouble with me. We can manage a convincing escape; he doesn't know I wasn't brought here against my will. We can fix the computer so that when we come out of the jump, the coordinates of Ekklesia are erased. There will be no risk. Besides, with my position I'll have access to information you could never reach.'

The truth of her reasoning was irrefutable.

'It seems the Lord can even use our weaknesses. But I have had to pay a price. I've seen a lot in nine years serving the Empire. That I can't face again. This time I won't be alone. I will work with the Church on Titan and, if I go there, on Earth. It's the only way.'

He could not protest. She had delayed telling him until she knew she had the strength to give him hope, the strength to go back. Now his hope would only die with him. He could not deny the chance of its fulfilment that she was offering.

'I'll come for you, Tanya. I'll come for you both.'

She turned to look out of the window and started. 'I wonder what he wants?'

'Who?'

'That man there,' she replied, indicating a figure striding across the spaceport bay away from them. He looked: there was only one person in sight – the Violet Knight, walking over to where the *New England* had docked. He disappeared inside the craft, the only one not securely grounded and moments later the full realization hit Paul. The second traitor, the one within the Inner Circle, was the Violet Knight. He was about to leave the planet city.

He checked his shield and baraq in his belt and made a dash for the door, but had hardly pulled it open when the roar of engines echoed out across the launch area. A technician ran over from an adjoining hangar.

'Who on earth's taking that bird up?'

Paul shouted above the noise of the thrusters, 'It's the Violet Knight; he's the traitor. We've got to stop him.' He made to pass by, but the other held him back.

'Steady on, you can't get near him now. He won't get far anyway.'

'What do you mean he won't get far?' Paul shot the question at him angrily. 'He'll head straight for Titan and then bring them all back here; the coordinates are still programmed into the ship's computers.'

'Oh no, he won't,' the other assured him with a certainty that startled him.

'What do you mean, he won't? What is there to stop him?'

'There's no hyperdrive unit, that's what. At least – not one that works.'

Paul laughed in exasperation. 'You're joking. We only came in on that ship about an hour ago. There's nothing wrong with it at all.'

'In that case, it's a miracle you got here then, isn't it?

122

Certainly wasn't that hyperdrive, that's for sure. Sliced neatly from end to end it is.'

An image sprang to Paul Trentam's mind: of star patterns accelerating towards them; of Isaac shouting that there was a warning light on the hyperdrive; the third pursuit ship that had followed them out under Sun City before burning up; and of his finger poised over the button that would rocket them into oblivion. He also remembered the moment's anguish as he punched that button and had felt it resist his pressure, anguish that had dissolved into relief as they emerged from hyperspace in the same instant over Ekklesia. Then he had forgotten; now he was certain. That button had never gone down.

'It's impossible.'

'No, like I said; it's a miracle.'

He watched the spaceship rising slowly on its four thrusters and asked, 'What if he tries to jump?'

The technician turned to face him. 'He'll get halfway. The primary stages were intact, but the space-time transformers were ruined. He'll get all the relativistic effects and somewhere just below light speed, the whole thing will blow up.'

Already the ship was a mere speck, accelerating away from the planet city, and then it was gone. They waited, their eyes fixed on the point where it had vanished. All three saw the brief flicker of light, the shooting star that glimmered for a long moment as it plummeted through the heavens, a life extinguished.

Paul turned to Tanya. 'We'd better see the White Knight, and then go and take a look at Jonathan.'

32

In the cool, clean hospital room Jonathan lay pale, semi-conscious beneath clean sheets. Isaac and Irène, Mark, Paul and Tanya were standing or sitting waiting. The surgeon came in and motioned Isaac away from the bed. He spoke to the old man in subdued tones, which the others could not hear but whose content they guessed. The gash in his arm was not serious, but the wound the laser had burned into his body had passed through both liver and spleen. There was nothing to be done.

Isaac returned to the pillow. 'How is the pain, my son?'

Jonathan tried to smile. 'Easing a little.' His words were little louder than a whisper. His hand touched his father's and their eyes met. 'Tell me, Father.'

Isaac leaned over and swept back a lock of hair. Tears brimmed in his eyes, but his voice was steady and gentle.

'Today, you will be with the Lord, my boy . . .'

Jonathan's eyes closed; his father held his hand tightly.

'I'm frightened.' His eyes opened again. 'Talk to me, Father, and Mother, I want to see your face.' Irène moved closer and Isaac leaned forwards.

'Dear, dear Jonathan. Don't be afraid.' He looked down at the hand clasped in his and felt the grip begin to weaken. His own hand was trembling. 'My boy . . .' He fell silent; his eyes returned to his son's face. On the bandage around his left arm, a small, red spot of blood appeared.

'No one has ever seen his face, Father . . .' The words were calm, quiet, wondering, fearful. His eyelids closed slowly and still more slowly opened again.

A single tear dripped from Isaac's grey beard, and then another.

'There is no fear in love. Love drives it out.' Again his son's eyes closed. 'Jonathan. No one has greater love than the one who lays down his life for his friends. You have followed Him.'

The other's gaze was steady, but the eyelids flickered, hung quivering, unable to decide whether to open or close. A dampness appeared on his brow.

'Isaac?'

The old man gently took the weight of his head as his face turned towards the pillow, and caught his gaze once more.

'There is a place prepared, Jonathan, prepared for you. You will be with Him.'

'Father . . .' A single whispered word breathed into a sigh, and he lay still. Silence settled upon the room, the silence of sadness in parting, but also of peace.

SHAPE-SHIFTER:
THE NAMING OF PANGUR BÁN
The first in the Pangur Bán series

Fay Sampson

Deep in a dark cave in the Black Mountain, a witch
was plotting mischief: 'We need something small,
something sly, to carry a spell . . . and then we shall
see who reigns on the Black Mountain!'

Shape-Shifter, the kitten, is her victim. But,
before the charm is complete, he escapes. He finds
himself caught in a spell that has gone wrong and a
body that is not his own.

In blind panic, he brings disaster even to those
who want to help him. Only a greater power can
break the spell.

PANGUR BÁN, THE WHITE CAT
The second in the Pangur Bán series

Fay Sampson

The princess Finnglas is in the deadly grip of the evil
Sea Monster, deep down in the mysterious
underwater kingdom of the Sea Witch. And Niall
has been bewitched by the mermaids.

Pangur Bán, the white cat, is desperate. He must
rescue them – but how can he free them from
enchantment?

Only Arthmael can do it. But who is Arthmael?
Where is he? Can Pangur find him in time?

NOTHING EVER STAYS THE SAME

Peggy Burns

Why, why, did everything have to change?

For Sandie it meant a whole new life – with the mother she'd hardly seen since she was a small child. It wasn't just that they didn't get on: Sandie's mother hated music – the one thing Sandie loved most in the world, the talent she had inherited from her father. It looked like the end of all her ambitions . . .